FAMILY

FAMILY
BOOK 5 OF THE DREAMHEALERS SAGA

M. C. A. HOGARTH

STUDIO
MCAH

mcahogarth.org

Family
Book 5 of The Dreamhealers Saga
First edition, copyright 2018 by M.C.A. Hogarth

M. Hogarth
PMB 109
4522 West Village Dr.
Tampa, FL 33624

ISBN-13: 978-1987730654
ISBN-10: 1987730658

Cover art by MCA Hogarth

Designed & typeset by Catspaw DTP Services
http://www.catspawdtp.com/

Author's Note

This third edition of "Family," the final story in the Dreamhealers saga, corrects several typos and addresses a handful of continuity errors. Readers will also enjoy the backmatter, which I have expanded in keeping with the style of the rest of the series. Enjoy!

T HE MINDLINE HAD GONE BLANK. Not as if it had been cut . . . but an imitation, complete with soft hissing white noise . . . the background noise of the universe, as imagined by another mind.

Vasiht'h looked up from the hot chocolate he was making in their abbreviated kitchen. When the mindline didn't swell back to its normal state, he poked his head out the door, feathered ears flaring. "Jahir? Is something wrong?"

His Eldritch partner was seated in front of their comm screen, which had gone dark. He was breathing: Vasiht'h could just see the lift of broad shoulders against the fine white hair that fell past them to the man's ribs. But otherwise, he was so still he might as well have been a statue. Vasiht'h tried again. "Jahir?"

"Oh, mm? Sorry." The Eldritch twisted a little in his seat to face him. "I didn't hear you."

"Apparently," Vasiht'h said, padding into the room, paws hushed on the carpet. "Are you okay? The mindline blanked."

"God and Lady, did it?" Jahir said, recovering his sense of humor. Vasiht'h watched animation return to that face, one he'd known for so many years now: human in seeming with a strong jaw and high cheekbones, but with skin pale as salt and eyes so deep a yellow they neared orange. Not human, Jahir, but Eldritch: an esper species rare and xenophobic and almost never found off their world. But this Eldritch had left his, and he was Vasiht'h's.

As far as Vasiht'h was concerned, anyway. He prodded the mindline that connected them gently until some color and life bloomed in it.

"Right," Jahir said, and drew in a deep breath. "How do you feel about a vacation?"

"Away from the starbase?" Vasiht'h asked, catching a whiff of exotic perfume and a hint of green things from their connection.

"Away from the starbase," Jahir agreed. "In fact . . . all the way home."

Vasiht'h stared at him.

Jahir returned to contemplation of the comm screen. "My mother has sent me a message . . . one of my cousins is to be wed. She would like as much of the family to attend as possible."

"I . . . I'd love to go," Vasiht'h said. "But . . . did the invitation include me? I didn't think aliens were welcome on your world."

"Not usually," Jahir agreed. "But I've spoken of you, of course, when I wrote home, and my mother specifically mentioned you coming."

Vasiht'h tried to figure out what was going on in his partner's head. The mindline remained devoid of anything but that tantalizing fragrance and hint of green. Nor did he see anything in the Eldritch's face. "You," he said after a moment, ". . . are blocking something?"

"Not . . . precisely," Jahir said. He ran a hand over his head, hair hissing away from his hand as it swung back in place. "I honestly don't know what to think. I have not been home in so long . . ." He blew out a breath and offered a lopsided smile. "There is a reason I left."

"You didn't like it," Vasiht'h said, letting his centauroid haunches settle and refolding the wings that covered his second back. "I'd guessed as much."

"But it would be good to see family," Jahir said. "Some of

them, at least. And Mother would not have asked, had she not thought it important for me to attend."

Vasiht'h sampled the new taste in the mindline between them. "She misses you."

"I think she might," Jahir agreed.

"Well, if you really think I'd be welcome . . ."

"I would like you to come," Jahir said, the mindline saturating with a smell like nostalgia: Vasiht'h's mind rendered it as the pine-amber scent of the oil his grandfather had worked into wood while polishing it. "It would be a hint of normalcy, you know, amid my relations."

Vasiht'h eyed him. "You're not making me feel better about this."

Jahir laughed. "That makes two of us." He lifted his brows. "You are not excited about being the first Glaseah to visit the world of the reclusive Eldritch?"

"Maybe a little," Vasiht'h admitted. "And maybe a little worried. When do we leave?"

Jahir said, "One week."

One week was long enough to reschedule their regular clients and hang out a virtual sign indicating they'd be gone. He and Jahir worked on Starbase Veta as xenotherapists, seeing to a multicultural, multi-species community rife with opportunities for misunderstanding, heartbreak, confusion and friction. They had been plying their trade for almost a decade already, and they were well-known; people came from all the way across a starbase the size of a moon to fall asleep on their couch and allow the two of them to walk into their subconscious minds and learn what there was to be found there.

When Vasiht'h had left his own homeworld to attend the college of xenopsychiatry on Seersana, he had not imagined he would end up at the side of an Eldritch. No doubt no one else would have thought to pair them either. He was one of the Glaseah, as different from a bipedal humanoid as was nearly possible in the Alliance: short, four-footed centauroid with small wings on his second back and a coat of black fur striped down the back in white. Different in custom, also; the Glaseah spoke mind-to-mind with little thought, and slept curled around one another, touched and indulged in behavior that, from everything Vasiht'h had heard, the Eldritch would have found appalling: too intimate by far and vulgar to boot. And yet, here he was . . . an Eldritch's chosen companion, standing alongside him at one of the thousands of docking facilities in the enormous base, awaiting their ride.

"So how does this work?" he asked, suppressing the urge to recheck the buckles on his saddlebags. They were snugged to his barrel behind the wing joints and very comfortable, but Vasiht'h had always been a fidgeter and this situation was tailor-made for twitching.

"If all goes as planned," Jahir said, "we shall be dropped off. We stay for the wedding . . . and then we come home. With a little socializing after the wedding, if company permits."

"That sounds so expected," Vasiht'h muttered.

"How would it not be?" Jahir asked, his amusement tinting the mindline sunlit yellow.

"I don't even know where your world *is*," Vasiht'h pointed out. "In fact, almost no one does . . ."

"The *Daughter's Promise* has docked," the docking slip's computer interrupted. "Passengers report to Bay 12 for embarkation."

"That's our ship," Jahir said, shifting his bag more comfortably over his shoulder and heading down the arrow painted on the floor with a twelve.

Mystified, Vasiht'h followed. Bay 12 looked like all the rest: a slick, technological antechamber, paneled in gray and silver with wallscreens showing boarding schedules and a view of the ship outside the bay. Vasiht'h glanced at it as they entered: a sleek courier-style vessel emblazoned with its name and a peculiar emblem, like an inverted U with twin triangles mounted on its apex.

A female Tam-illee foxine was awaiting them, dressed in

what looked like livery: dark blue with silver piping, with her ship's emblem embroidered at her breast. She was a pretty youth, bright gold with brown ears and eyes, and on seeing Jahir she bowed. "Lord Seni Galare."

/*She knows you,*/ Vasiht'h murmured through the mindline, surprised.

/*She would,*/ Jahir answered, muted. /*It's her job.*/ To the Tam-illee he said, "Navigatrix."

"If you'll step through the airlock, my lord," the woman said, ears perked. "We're scheduled for departure in twenty minutes."

"Thank you," Jahir said gravely, and headed through the airlock door. Vasiht'h followed him, struggling with his questions. He chose one of the lot and murmured, "Does she know you?"

"Not personally," Jahir replied. "But Eldritch, she does know. She is in the Queen's employ."

"Your Queen has employees? Alien ones?" Vasiht'h asked, astonished.

Jahir smiled at him, just a twitch of his lips, and Vasiht'h desisted. He tried very hard to respect his partner's reticence; he even knew the habit of secrecy about their race had a name among the Eldritch, the Veil. Prodding Jahir about an issue that triggered that secrecy sometimes netted him answers, or sometimes none, along with his partner's agitation. It wasn't always worth the trouble. It certainly wasn't here, when there were easier ways to get the information he wanted.

The inside of the vessel was very comfortable: not meant for multiple passengers, Vasiht'h thought immediately. The section usually devoted to rows of seats had been converted into something that looked more like a living room, with two chairs around a table set against the wall beneath the viewport; on the other side, a bench and a coffee table. Aft of it was a door that led into a bunkroom. While it was no more luxurious than any other high-end private Alliance vessel Vasiht'h had seen, the style of the furnishings was different: more baroque than typical. Deeper and more vibrant colors: burgundy, violet, burnt ochre, sky blue and silver. Real wood finish on the panels . . . he trailed his fingers over it surreptitiously and felt the oil used to condition it.

Jahir stowed his luggage in the bunkroom and without asking helped Vasiht'h with his bags, then returned aft . . . to unpack? Would they be in transit that long? Vasiht'h sat in the living room, tail curled over his paws, and waited for the Tamillee to return.

When she did, she sealed off the door to the airlock. "That's that," she said with satisfaction. "We'll be off in ten minutes, alet."

The formal name for 'friend' set him at ease, despite the peculiarity of the circumstance. "Thank you," he said. "I'm Vasiht'h. You are?"

"Livia Navigatrix, of the Queen's Tams," she said proudly.

"That . . . has got to be a story," Vasiht'h said.

"It is!" she answered. "And if you want, I'll tell it to you while I do the pre-flight checks."

"I would be delighted," Vasiht'h said.

Sitting in the fore of the ship with Livia after their successful departure, Vasiht'h listened to the story with growing incredulity. When she finished her recitation, he said, "So . . . let's see if I heard this correctly. Your many generations-past ancestress was friends with an Eldritch spy, and he enlisted the aid of her daughter and her daughter's husband to set up a secure courier service between the Alliance and the Eldritch homeworld."

"That's right," Livia said, sitting easily at the helm.

"And for generations, your family has been running shuttles to the Eldritch homeworld," Vasiht'h said.

"Yes," Livia said, grinning. "Ever since the very first Navigator of the Queens' Tams took the helm on behalf of Queen Liolesa Galare." She leaned over and added, "Mind you, we met up with Lord Meriaen Jisiensire before Liolesa was queen. His sovereign was Maraesa, who would never have heard of such a thing. She wanted him to spy for her, not to foster any longer-lasting ties.

Liolesa now, she's a different kind."

"I imagine she must be," Vasiht'h said, amazed.

"She's the one who decided to employ us this way, because Heather SecurestheFuture married a pilot and made the case to her through Lord Meriaen Jisiensire that we could provide this service. She thought it was a fine idea, and even gave us our own name: the Queens' Tams." She tapped the emblem. "It's a horse-shoe. With Tam-illee ears! I understand the Queen has a sense of humor."

"A horseshoe!" Vasiht'h said, chuckling. "I guess the love of horses is endemic to the species."

"It seems so," Livia agreed, comfortable.

"How many generations has it been, then?" Vasiht'h asked.

"Nine," Livia said. She grinned. "You want to know the crazi-est part?"

"What's that?" Vasiht'h asked, wondering how the entire story hadn't already been the craziest part.

"The lord's still alive," Livia said, shaking her head. "Can you imagine? Nine generations of us, and he's still around."

"That . . . does surprise me," Vasiht'h admitted slowly. He didn't like the reminder that Jahir would outlive him handily, barring any accident. The Glaseah were long-lived among the Pelted, but even the healthiest member of his species could only expect a century and a half of life.

"That would be Heather's doing," Livia said, nodding. "She accused him of planning to abandon us because her mother Sydnie had died."

"That hardly seems fair," Vasiht'h murmured. "I can't imagine living long enough to see someone die, and then still remaining with their children."

"By her way of thinking, there was no reason to hurt the chil-dren who'd grown up with him around just because their mother and father had died," Livia said, leaning forward to check the course. Her fingers flickered easily over the board. "So he's stuck around for all nine generations, and he's with us still. Sort of a family fixture."

The idea troubled Vasiht'h; he imagined an heirloom passed on from generation to generation, forever immured in its household, except that the heirloom was a living being.

"I can tell by your face that you think it's awful," Livia said, her voice softening. "But you know what the Eldritch call us among themselves, Vasiht'h-alet? 'Mortals.' They know how fast we live, compared to them. They choose to put a distance between us because of it. But how fair is that to us? To say that we're not worth knowing just because we die quicker? I mean, would you not love someone, even if you knew they had some terminal disease that would kill them in five years?"

"No," Vasiht'h said slowly, drawing the word out. "Of course not."

"Why not?" she asked.

"Because . . ." He trailed off. "That's different."

"Is it?" she asked. She returned her attention to her controls. "Lesandural Meriaen Jisiensire might put the dirt on my grave in seventy years, alet. But the Queens' Tams clan will always be there for him, year after year. That has to mean something . . . or he would have left a long time ago."

———— ❧ ————

"This is crazy," Vasiht'h murmured several days later as the vessel began its final approach to his partner's homeworld . . . at last. "I had no idea just flying to your world would be this . . . convoluted a process."

"And that was the easy part," Jahir said, belting himself into the safety harness. "Just wait until you see what we have to do to achieve my parents' house."

"Let me guess," Vasiht'h said. "It doesn't involve something as sensible as Padding down to their front porch."

"Try 'landing at the planet's sole spaceport and riding several days across the countryside'," Jahir said.

Vasiht'h stared at him, the mindline thick with the static of his stunned disbelief.

"Which part has you more incredulous," Jahir said with

weary amusement, "the spaceport? Or the travel?"

"You have one spaceport to serve the entire planet?" Vasiht'h said finally, choosing the most obvious. "One single spaceport?"

"And a small one at that," Jahir said. "A day's ride from the capital, more or less. It is the Queen's private facility. She uses it to receive visitors to the world, and to occasionally leave it herself." He lifted a hand at Vasiht'h's shocked-orange response, spilling like paint through their connection. "Yes, she leaves. That would be a family secret, though the Tams know. Of course, since they're the ones who ferry her around. They're not just for those of us who have left the world."

"Your Queen uses a private service to jet around the Alliance," Vasiht'h said. And then, gathering his incredulous thoughts, "She *sneaks* around the Alliance?"

"More or less," Jahir said. "For official state visits she allows the Alliance to assign her the proper escorts. But she does not always wish to be known."

Vasiht'h continued staring at him.

"As for the travel, well . . . one spaceport. The Tams could land anywhere, but they have been asked only to use the spaceport, to minimize their intrusiveness. You have long known my people are xenophobes. The sight of outworlders would hardly be tolerated." He drew in a breath and let it out slowly. "And while the Tams could drop us off somewhere closer, the shuttle would still have to remain out of sight of the house. We would have a long walk."

"And they wouldn't anyway," Vasiht'h guessed. "Because they've promised otherwise."

"Just so," Jahir said, leaning back in his chair and closing his eyes.

Vasiht'h studied the face of his partner, unnerved and trying to tamp it before it reached the mindline. He must have failed because Jahir said, without moving or opening his eyes, "Ask."

"Why are you telling me all this now?" Vasiht'h said, disturbed. "You've always been reticent to share these things. You told me about the Veil—"

"—and yet here we are," Jahir said, looking at him then, just a slight movement of his head, white lashes casting shadows over amber eyes. "You go now to the center of the mystery, arii. There won't be any hiding things from you. I do not know why my mother asked you to come by name, but she did. I suspect . . . something may be afoot, and I don't know what it might be . . . but in any case, you will leave here with your own Veil to keep. It won't be my secret anymore. It will be ours." He closed his eyes, and a soft velvet feel suffused the mindline, gentle as new snow falling. "Finally. I won't have to keep secrets from you anymore."

Watching the lines ease from Jahir's face, Vasiht'h said, "Maybe . . . that's why she did it."

"Maybe," Jahir said, though the velvet became mist, and then a storm-wind blew through it, carrying uncertainty and unease.

"Twenty minutes to landing," came Livia's voice. "Fasten your harnesses, alet, lord."

It was not an unpleasant world, Vasiht'h thought—fortunately, since he was forced to tramp through it on his own four paws. His partner had the benefit of an animal . . . though admittedly, taking care of it seemed tedious.

It surely helped that it was spring, and there was birdsong in every tree, and the hills were softly felted with bright grass and dotted with tiny flowers, white like sugar and blond like champagne. The sun on his back was warm and gentle, a far cry from his own homeworld's more tropical brilliance. The colors here felt kinder, watercolors to Anseahla's oils.

His partner's mood had cleared, also. Something about the journey, the horse, the physical exertion and the environment had soothed him. The mindline was thick with pleasing tastes and smells and fragments of memories, so fleeting they reminded Vasiht'h of distant birds against high clouds.

"You seem happy," he said, finally.

"It's the wild," Jahir said. His hands were resting lightly on the pommel of the saddle, the reins loose in his fingers. "I had some of my best times out here."

Vasiht'h caught a flicker of shapes in the mindline. "With people?"

Jahir glanced at him. "Am I leaking so much?"

"Maybe a little," Vasiht'h said. "Probably inevitable, given where we are."

"Probably," Jahir agreed, drawing in a deep breath. "Yes, with people. My brother, Sernataila, and my cousin, Sediryl."

"Your brother, and your cousin," Vasiht'h said carefully.

"I have not spoken of them much . . . or at all," Jahir said. "Though I suppose the mindline has revealed me, now and then." He exhaled. "We parted under less than ideal terms. Sediryl . . . well. The less said about that, the better. And I don't know where Amber is at any given moment, for he is a far traveler and a poor correspondent. Maybe he'll have come . . . that would be good, I think. To see him again."

"But not your cousin," Vasiht'h said.

"Sediryl does not have a high opinion of us as a species," Jahir said, voice growing tight with discomfort.

There was something in that sending that struck Vasiht'h as strange, somehow. Some color: flushed incarnadine, glazed like the paint on porcelain. But he did not ask. "How far are we now?"

"We'll be there this afternoon," Jahir said.

"Four days," Vasiht'h murmured. "And we've not seen another Eldritch. Are you so sparsely settled then?"

"You could say that," Jahir said, wry. Then, more seriously, "We are not exactly populous. Probably for the best, given how long we live, or we'd have carpeted the world from end to end by now."

"Are you serious?" Vasiht'h asked, unable to tell. "Or rationalizing your own ambivalence about family?"

For a long moment, Jahir stared at the vista before them, his eyes unfocused. Then he chuckled. "A little of both, mayhap."

Vasiht'h sighed. "I sympathize."

Jahir glanced at him. "Ah? This is something new." He lifted a brow. "You keeping some secret from me, as well?"

"Not so much keeping secret as not wanting to think of it too much myself," Vasiht'h said. "I'm reaching the age where I am subject to messages strongly suggesting I come home and add to the genepool."

Jahir frowned, resettling himself on the horse and looking more closely at his partner. "This *is* new. When did this start?"

"About half a year ago," Vasiht'h said. "When I had my birthday." At Jahir's scrutiny, he lifted his hands. "It's not specific. Literally. We all get messages once we hit a certain age. Males are asked to consider sperm donation, or to visit the local *kis't*. Females are asked to donate eggs. All of us get lectures about the benefits of family life."

"Then . . . that woman on the base? The one who invited you to dinner . . ."

"Had gotten her own note, yes," Vasiht'h said. "She wanted to know if I was willing to donate. Said that I was successful, xenophilic, and healthy, and thought I would make a good match."

"And I had teased you so," Jahir said. "I am sorry, arii. I would not have, had I known it would be so . . . awkward."

"Awkward," Vasiht'h said with a grimace. "I guess it is that. But we were engineered with low sex drives, and some of us don't have any at all. None of us have children by accident. We choose it with a life partner, or we're reminded to do it. But it's entirely artificial, the maintenance of our population." He smiled lopsidedly. "It takes work. Like all relationships and communities do."

"I admit I had never thought through the implications of your lack of . . . interest," Jahir said slowly.

Vasiht'h snorted. "You? O celibate one? Surely you jest."

"I'm not without feelings," Jahir said. "Just . . . ah . . . there are extenuating circumstances."

"Like what?" Vasiht'h said, careful, because he'd often wondered but never felt at liberty to ask. Not like he did here, when Jahir confessed he need not keep secrets anymore.

His partner had colored. "Like age," he said. "I am no longer young, that any pretty thing will turn my head."

"Or there's some particular pretty thing you're saving yourself for?" Vasiht'h said, off-hand, and was completely unprepared for how quickly the mindline went dark. "Jahir! Goddess . . . I'm sorry. Did I offend?"

"No, no," Jahir said, touching a gloved knuckle to his brow. "Just . . ." He flushed. "Not a subject I am comfortable discussing." He sighed, smiled. "It's not you, Vasiht'h. Just . . . we've come home, and to attend a wedding, and I am having to face all these matters again. I, no more than you, like pressure, but here among us having more than one child is considered proof of unusual fertility and my mother had two of us. There is a great deal of speculation about whether I inherited her . . . vigor."

"Just you? What about your brother?" Vasiht'h asked, wide-eyed.

"He is subject to the same speculation," Jahir said, a sour lemon taste filtering through the mindline. "Or why do you suppose both of us have vanished from family affairs? I pledge you, it was not curiosity about the outworld alone that spurred us both away."

"Nothing like it," Vasiht'h said, rueful, "family."

"No," Jahir said. He glanced at his partner. "That woman . . . would you consider . . . did you. . . ."

"No," Vasiht'h said, without meeting his gaze. Across the mindline there was nothing, just a blank that soaked emotion like cotton. "I told her I wanted to be involved in the lives of my children, and that I wasn't ready yet. And she definitely wasn't the right person."

There seemed no good reply to that, so Jahir spoke none until the path hove into view. His horse's hooves struck packed earth as he guided it up the embankment and onto level ground. "We are nearly arrived."

Vasiht'h scrabbled up after him, digging claws into the earth as he climbed. He brushed off his fur once he reached the path, regretting the day's dirt on his legs. He would have liked to arrive glossy and picture-perfect, having some suspicion of how susceptible the Eldritch were to appearances from some few hints Jahir had let slip over their long partnership. Those same hints were all he had to prepare him for his partner's house.

. . . they were not sufficient preparation to clear the forest and find something Vasiht'h would have called a palace, from its size and opulence. Even years of arguing with Jahir over money, and knowing that the Eldritch was rich, could not have inspired his imagination to produce an edifice this magnificent. That was the only way to describe it. Normal people lived in houses. This was an *edifice*.

"Here we are," Jahir said. "My family's country seat."

"Your family's *country* seat?" Vasiht'h repeated, incredulous. "How big is the non-country version?"

Jahir glanced down at him, then said, "Oh, no . . . no you have a misconception. The family's city presence is smaller, more like a . . . a townhouse, one of many on the Nobles' Row."

Only slightly mollified, Vasiht'h aligned himself as close to Jahir as he could without distressing the horse. They were walking down what felt like an infinitely long path among topiaries and waist-height hedge mazes—hedge mazes!—and ornamental gardens toward the multi-winged building at the path's end, a stately pile of gray and pale stone that Vasiht'h imagined must require a fleet of servants to maintain and clean. He was not well enough acquainted with architecture styles to know what it reminded him of, but it was encrusted with statues and columns and friezes that, had they been any other color than white, would have been utterly overwhelming. As it was, from a distance the whole thing reminded him of some kind of wedding cake. An extremely expensive one.

"I knew you were rich, but not this rich," Vasiht'h murmured finally as the path went on . . . and on . . . and on . . . and the estate seemed to grow no closer.

Jahir's voice was uncomfortable. "I would not draw any conclusions."

"Jahir?" Vasiht'h said, unable to help the tension in his voice. "Are you making a joke? Can you see this place? Are you actually looking at it?"

"Appearances aren't everything. Speaking of which . . ."

They were coming upon a garden: an occupied one. Spread across the lawn were several Eldritch ladies in dresses so voluminous Vasiht'h thought it fortuitous they were seated, as he could hardly imagine walking in them. They were companioned by an equal number of males, in coats somewhat less ostentatious, but only just. They were arranged in a rough circle around a single male, who was reading from a book. A very rough circle: if they were courting couples, Vasiht'h would never have guessed from how much space they kept between them.

It was useless to think they'd go unnoticed, even with Vasiht'h safely hidden on the other side of Jahir's tall gray horse. One of the women waved to him and then the whole group was rising.

The first woman called to Jahir, and the single word she used was so long and so unintelligible that Vasiht'h could hardly believe she had formed it so easily with what looked like a merely mortal mouth. He had not had much chance to hear the Eldritch language; what little of it he knew had come from Jahir's dreaming mind, or from occasional slipped thoughts through the mindline. He had no idea it was so . . . he licked his teeth. Thick. Drippy. Flowery. It felt like eating flowers—

—no, the mindline was giving him that feeling. That, and a translation. He strained his feathered ears forward, unable to help the reflex even though the words he could understand were echoing in his head, not in his ears.

". . . so good to see you again, milord, it has been so long."

Not long enough, was the strong thought that shivered the mindline. But the words Jahir actually spoke meant, ". . . it certainly does feel so, my lady cousin."

"Will you be staying?" she was asking, leaning on the fence and smiling at him in a way that Vasiht'h found profoundly discomfiting . . . as if sizing him up for stud duty. "It would be a great pleasure to renew our acquainta—Goddess and Lord what is *that!*"

Her squeal was so distressed Vasiht'h jumped and looked for whatever had upset her . . . only to realize she was staring at *him*, and so was the rest of her party. Their expressions made him wonder if his travel through the countryside had spread him with something more unsavory than dirt.

"This," Jahir said, "is my partner and truest friend, Vasiht'h."

"Your partner?" she said, and the mindline spread that translation with scarlet in a way that made Vasiht'h's skin crawl. "Not that kind of partner!" he interrupted, dismayed.

They all looked at him, with shock and distaste. Vasiht'h colored beneath his dark pelt, grateful that his blush wasn't visible.

"It speaks," one of the males said, the translation swirled in shadows. "In Universal, is it? The tongue of mortals."

"Yes," Jahir said, dry, "one would expect a citizen of the Alliance to speak Universal. I seem to recall you once had lessons in it yourself, Bashinal. Or have you lost your facility?"

The longer he listened, the more he heard the colors. Jahir's also: there was something wicked and black in the last few sentences, something that gleamed like steel.

"I hardly had reason to maintain it," the male answered with a sniff.

"Come," Jahir said to Vasiht'h, nudging the horse. "My lady mother expects us."

"Right," Vasiht'h said, shoulders tight. As they walked away, he muttered, "Am I right in thinking you're snubbing them by cutting off the conversation?"

"Some things are universal," Jahir responded, voice low. "I am sorry, arii. I did not expect to be waylaid before our arrival in the house, amid my family and retainers. You will find them more agreeable."

"So that's not the kind of thing I should expect? The open prejudice is unusual? And what's with the colors?"

A long pause, pained in the mindline like a nerveless limb. "Would that it were so. My family is among the most liberal in all the world; excepting one other family, we are the most likely to embrace the outworld, both its peoples and its ideas," Jahir said. "But that doesn't mean we fail of our share of bad seeds.

My cousin is marrying into a far more parochial House. More typical of Eldritch than the Galare. Many of them will be here for the wedding." He paused. "Did you say . . . colors? You heard the colors?"

"Saw them more like," Vasiht'h said, and tweaked the mind-line. "Through here."

"Ah," Jahir said. "Of course." He smiled a little, lopsided. "Our language can be modified for nuance, and the modes are named for colors."

"They're certainly very expressive," Vasiht'h said. "I didn't like half the things they were implying if I was reading any of it right."

"I did not think of the language problem," Jahir murmured, frowning. "I'm glad the mindline appears to be attending to that for us."

"As long as we're listening to the same person," Vasiht'h guessed. "That means if I end up alone or if you're paying attention to something else, I might not get anything. Is there no one who speaks Universal?"

"Or who will admit it?" Jahir said, tired. At the Glaseah's sharp glance, he said, "Oh yes. Most of us learned in childhood by the Queen's decree. But one must practice a skill to maintain it over centuries of life . . . and to do that, one must value it."

"Maybe," Vasiht'h said slowly, "you should have left me at home."

Jahir looked down at him, pained.

———∞∞∞———

Approaching the manor did nothing to assuage Vasiht'h's growing sense of unease. The softly splashing fountain in the courtyard, the opulence of the facade, the broad, shallow steps leading up to the doors, which were well and again large enough to admit not just himself, but five of him abreast . . . it was overwhelming. He had assumed Jahir to be titled, having caught some of the university registrars referring to him as 'Lord Seni Galare' when they first met . . . but he was not at all prepared for the implications of the wealth and size of his partner's family estate. This was something for one of his sister's romance novels, not for real people. It was profoundly discomfiting to find himself in the middle of it, wondering when the caricatured villain would show and fearing it might be him.

The youth that appeared to take Jahir's horse only stared at the Glaseah, at least, but did not speak. Distressed to find that minimal courtesy a relief, Vasiht'h followed the Eldritch to the door and through it, into a towering foyer, a hemispherical room lined with statues set into alcoves and illuminated by an enormous lacy chandelier . . . a chandelier with candles. Shocked into staring at it, Vasiht'h missed the murmur of conversation that sent servants scurrying away.

He was still wondering whether anyone ever worried about candle wax dripping on their heads when he felt the flush of affection through the mindline, so warm and deep it was like drinking wine. Old wine. There before him was his partner . . . holding the hands of a woman in an outrageous display of intimacy between Eldritch, who never touched. In her face Jahir's crisp features were softened, and age had traced lines beneath her eyes. But she was lovely, and there was a great peace about her. Vasiht'h relaxed despite himself.

"Vasiht'h," Jahir said in Universal. "My lady mother, Jeasa Seni Galare. Mother, here is my partner of long association, of whom I have spoken so much."

"Vasiht'h," the woman said, smiling and offering her hands to him in turn. Surprised, he took them, and with them a feather-soft mental touch, like a benison. Her Universal was softly accented but perfectly understandable, and she spoke with quiet confidence. "I have read about you with such pleasure over the years. You have honored our house by accepting our invitation, and delighted me personally by coming. I have long wanted to meet you."

"Ma'am," Vasiht'h said, blushing again. "I'm pleased to make your acquaintance."

She smiled at him, then touched Jahir again, on the arm this time. "No doubt you are both weary from the journey. I have had your room prepared, my son, and made arrangements for your guest."

"Thank you," Jahir said. "We wouldn't mind the opportunity to wash up before supper."

"Go on then," she said, smiling. "The packs off your horse should already be there. If you wish, you can join me in the salon afterward."

"Nothing would please me more, my lady," Jahir answered. /This way,/ he murmured to Vasiht'h and set off. Bewildered, Vasiht'h followed through a succession of ever more luxurious rooms. He caught a glance of himself in one of the mirror-lined corridors: sadly, he looked as stunned as he felt.

His partner's rooms—the plural was accurate—were up several flights of stairs, and comprised a parlor, which shared a fireplace with a sleeping chamber, a study lined with books, and a bath. The entirety of the suite was hung with tapestries and impressive paintings, portraits and inevitable depictions of horses . . . the floors were thick with rugs which, if his paw pads were any judge, were woven of some kind of silk fiber. There was a harpsichord in the parlor that Vasiht'h was afraid to ask the age of, an orrery that appeared to be ornamented with precious gems, and the bed in the sleeping chamber was a monument, large enough to sleep three or four Eldritch, be-curtained and lavish with brocade covers and mounds of pillows. It was also high enough that it came with a miniature step-stool painted with flowers and leafed in silver.

Vasiht'h stood in the center of this finery, dusty with four days' worth of grime and wearing a perfectly serviceable but rather worn set of packs, and felt like the lowest and drabbest menial in a fairy tale palace.

"Ah . . . I . . . suppose I should have warned you about all this," Jahir said, folding his arms and looking down.

"Yes, you could have," Vasiht'h answered. And then, more normally, "Though to be fair, I don't think being warned would have really helped." He looked at his partner, who was leaning against the wall beside one of the windows—the panels were propped open, and they were made of stained glass. "Aksivaht'h's *breath*, Jahir! Why . . . why did you leave this? I had no idea you were . . . were . . ."

"What?" Jahir asked, voice low. "You have asked me before, you know. About money."

"This isn't just money!" Vasiht'h exclaimed. "This is . . . this is ridiculous! Goddess, arii, you have . . . you have an estate, and servants and . . . your private gardens are the size of our entire neighborhood on Veta!"

"Technically they're not mine," Jahir said. "They are my mother's, and will remain so for centuries, barring misfortune."

"But this is your house!"

"Yes," Jahir said slowly. "This is my family house. And yes, it will be mine at some point. And I left it because . . . I had to, Vasiht'h."

The bell that sang through the mindline beneath those words was clear and deep and bone-shivering. Startled, Vasiht'h met his eyes.

"I had to, Vasiht'h. I needed the Alliance. Wanted work that meant something, wanted the interplay of cultures and ideas and lives. Wanted . . . the vibrancy of living out there." Jahir looked out the window, his yearning urgent enough to turn Vasiht'h toward the view by force. "I shall live another dozen centuries. I cannot imagine doing so here, where nothing changes. Where my only chance of seeing an unfamiliar face is if any of my peers are fortunate enough to beget a new generation, and that a rarity. Even then, it's not the same. It's not . . . random, the way my life is with you." He turned back to Vasiht'h. "There's no serendipity here. Nothing unexpected. Sometimes I fear there never will be."

"You hate it," Vasiht'h said, genuinely surprised at the thickness of the feeling in the mindline.

"Utterly, and how it pains me to say so!" Jahir drew in a breath. "For I love this world, and yet I cannot bear it. When you met me, I said I wasn't sure what I was doing on Seersana, and I could not imagine what I should do when I finished school. Every

word of that was true, arii. Because my life here had never prepared me to consider a life that wasn't scripted."

"You escaped," Vasiht'h murmured. "And before it could
become habit. That inability to imagine a different future."

"There is no fortune on this earth or any other worth the loss
of that plasticity," Jahir said.

"Goddess!" Vasiht'h said. "What are the rest of the Eldritch
like, if they *have* lost it?"

"I fear you are about to find out," Jahir said, low.

For a moment, Vasiht'h said nothing, listening to the quality
of the silence between them and finding it unsettling. Then
he said, "Well, I'd better clean up if we're going to go see your
mother." He started unbuckling his packs. "Will I see your father
too?"

"That would be a trick, since he has been in his grave since
Amber was a babe in swaddling clothes," Jahir said, watching
him.

Vasiht'h looked up. "I'm—"

"—it's an old sorrow," Jahir said. "Very old, trust me. I made
my peace with it a long time ago."

"Probably before I was born," Vasiht'h said, trying for a joke
and failing when Jahir answered.

"Very probably, yes."

Vasiht'h met his eyes, and Jahir allowed it. The mindline
between them was fallow, waiting for one of them to fill it.

"You wanted me to come here for this reason, didn't you,"
Vasiht'h said slowly. "So I could confront all these uncomfortable things about what you are and where you came from. It's
just like that time you decided we needed to take that vacation
on Seersana, with our quadmates, and made the arrangements,
just like that."

"I learned such quickness from you," Jahir said, leaning
against the bedchamber's door frame.

"Maybe," Vasiht'h said. "I'm not entirely sure. You make a lot
of plans without telling me, and long in advance. This is the same
thing, isn't it? You think it's time I knew all these things, and

your mother gave you the opening you needed."

"It was convenient," Jahir allowed, and the taste in the mindline then was bitter like char, and sad like a distant melody. "Arii . . . I don't think you understand how hard it is for us to stop . . . obfuscating. We live a long time. We become very adept at not revealing ourselves, until finally we don't know how to stop. You know how deeply engrained the habits of a lifetime are for one of you. Can you imagine the habits of a lifetime for one of us?"

"You needed help," Vasiht'h said. "Breaking the Veil."

"Yes," Jahir said simply. "And I have long wanted you under it, for to hide myself from you . . . it is a thorn. I am tired of suffering it. You deserve better; you have earned it."

Vasiht'h sat, heedless of the dirt on his haunches and the perfect silky rug under his rump. He studied his partner, and was permitted that study, and softened a little at what that permission implied. "Thank you," he said finally. "For wanting me to know."

"You are welcome," Jahir said, quiet, and through the mindline Vasiht'h felt something like the first sunlight of spring after a long, gray winter. "Now I shall help you with the facilities. I doubt you will like them overmuch."

"Since you'd never seen a shower until you left for the university, I fear you're right."

The salon Jahir's mother had invited them to was something out of a historical drama. A gracious rectangular room with great windows paneled in clear beveled glass, its stone walls were faced with pale wood and large green carpets softened their footsteps. Musical instruments were scattered throughout the salon: a harp taller than Vasiht'h; some kind of instrument with a keyboard, perhaps a piano or another harpsichord; and hanging on brackets on the wall, four stringed instruments of various sizes, bowed or plucked. The mindline brought Vasiht'h a whisper of sensation at his fingertips, strings cutting into tender fingers, and he wondered how many lessons his partner had had. Maybe in this very room?

The lady Jeasa was seated in one of the elegant, upholstered chairs, her skirts spread gracefully around her and a porcelain cup of surpassing delicacy in one small hand. Jahir bowed to her and Vasiht'h tried the same.

"Oh, won't you have tea?" she said, smiling at them. "It is still warm. And there are scones if you're so inclined."

"I may be," Vasiht'h murmured, wondering if she minded his informality. From her smile and her easy use of Universal, he guessed not and relaxed fractionally.

Jahir poured for them both, taking the cups to a low table set in the center of the grouping of chairs. There was enough space beside the one Jahir chose for Vasiht'h to settle, so he did, as neatly as possible, tail tucked around his paws and wings tightly folded. Bad enough that the tea cup felt so fragile in his hands . . . he'd hate to knock anything over.

The scone was delicious. Mildly sweet, crumbly, tender. The butter was so fresh it gave him gooseflesh. Vasiht'h applied himself to the food and to looking gracious while eating, as much as possible with a muzzle.

"Thank you for coming," Jeasa was saying to his partner. "I know you find such things wearisome, my son."

"I would find them less wearisome if the betrothed were old enough to know their own minds," Jahir said. "You'd think we would have left off with such barbarism when evidence of its continual failure to achieve the stated aims made it clear we are better off without it."

"Alas," she said. "We had best pray this time it works, for we need this wedding, and this alliance."

"Since when does the Galare need anything?" Jahir asked.

"Oh, Jahir," his mother said with a sigh. "You have been gone so long. You forget what it's like. Liolesa does not rule by fiat. She can be blocked . . . or deposed."

He snorted over his cup. "I should like to see anyone try."

"You may live to do so, if things continue as they are."

"You're talking about . . . your queen being overthrown?" Vasiht'h interjected, surprised.

"Yes," Jeasa said. "The very thing, friend Vasiht'h."

"But wouldn't that mean . . . a civil war?" Vasiht'h said, wondering how Jahir could be so calm about it.

"It would, if it were possible," Jahir said. "But a civil war would require many more Eldritch than are willing to take up arms against one another and shed blood. We are not great doers of deeds, arii. More dreamers of them."

"From your mouth to Aksivaht'h's ear," Vasiht'h said. "I would hate to see a civil war, any civil war, here or anywhere else." He looked up from his place. "If I may . . .what's got everyone so upset at your queen?"

"That," Jahir said, "would be you."

". . . me?"

"You," Jeasa agreed. "And others like you. And the Alliance, and what it can bring to us as a people. We are split very harshly on the matter, friend Vasiht'h. Some of us wish to embrace the outworld. We are sovereign allies of the Pelted, and yet we call on almost none of the treaty provisions. We ask no aid. We suffer no trade. We exchange no knowledge. We allow no visitation—"

"—no visitation!" Vasiht'h exclaimed, wondering suddenly if his presence was somehow illegal, and if that was why all the Tam-illee kept themselves so scarce.

"—with some exception," Jeasa finished. "However, we are sorely outnumbered by those who wish nothing to do with the outworld, who despise the alien and show contempt for all their works. And even though Liolesa is one of our number," she said, turning her attention back to Jahir, "she is not protected from the will of the majority. If she pushes hard enough, they will push back and we will lose all the ground we have gained. You've read my letters, my love. You know it's so. Matters grow ever more tense."

"The Queen must realize it," Jahir said, setting his tea cup aside. "She has survived this long, more than long enough to know how to gauge the tenor of her people."

"Mayhap," Jeasa said, but to Vasiht'h's ear she sounded unconvinced. "Even so, there is danger yet. And that is why we have a duty to her, to help her in her aims. Thus this marriage, arranged in the traditional way . . . so that your cousin has time to affect her betrothed. By the time they're grown, he will have been so exposed to her way of thinking that he will no longer question his own feelings on the matter of the outworld."

"Assuming he is the one affected," Jahir said. "It's as likely that he'll poison her with his small-mindedness."

"That I doubt," Jeasa said. "Children love the unusual and the unknown. The Alliance is full of fascinating and colorful beings. It will be enough to learn they exist. Natural curiosity will take care of the rest."

"You hope," Vasiht'h said, struggling to follow the conversation and not at all liking its gist.

"We hope," Jeasa agreed.

"Pardon me for saying so," Vasiht'h said after a long pause, "but this sounds like . . . a potentially explosive situation. If I understand right, you're bringing a very backward family in to marry to one of your people in the hopes of helping to affect some political change. And you invited me into the middle of it . . . why? To polarize things? It seems counter-productive."

"It sounds like a party to me!" said a new voice from the door. "Why, and to think I almost didn't come!"

The feel of a door slamming came through the mindline so powerfully Vasiht'h braced himself against it, feeling the wind on his back, the sound like a clout to the ears. It had shut on something but not fast enough to prevent the bright wash of scarlet from flooding his spine. It was no hyperbole that led Vasiht'h to claim his species was free of the tyranny of hormones, but even without direct experience he knew from walks through the dreams of clients what arousal was like and that . . . that was as powerful a brush with it as he'd ever felt—

—from Jahir?

Stunned, Vasiht'h looked up at the door to see what had inspired it, and saw a sylph in an orange gown, scandalously tight through the waist and breast, enough to show her narrow ribcage, the suggestion of thin hips, all things he would never have thought to notice and knew were his partner's observations. Her hair was perilously close to unbound with only a few braids to hold it back from her pointed face . . . and such eyes . . . ! Large orange eyes, thickly lashed and alive with dangerous passions.

She was beautiful, and sharp as storms on a horizon, and she took Vasiht'h's breath away through Jahir. He heard the whisper down the mindline.

/Sediryl . . ./

Jeasa was already standing to receive the girl with one of those so-intimate gestures, young hands clasped in old. "Sediryl! How wonderful to have you home again!"

"You are possibly the only one who could say so and mean it, aunt," Sediryl said in flawless Universal, without even the touch of an accent. She turned those secret-heavy eyes on Jahir and added, "Unless I can count you among them, cousin."

Jahir had also risen. He bowed, hair sliding over his shoulder to shroud his face. "Sediryl."

"I had no idea you'd be here," Sediryl said, and looked at Vasiht'h. "And with such interesting company. You are?"

"Vasiht'h," he answered, near paralyzed by Jahir's reaction, even with that shut door in the mindline keeping all but the smallest of leaks from escaping. "Jahir's partner."

"You? His partner?" Sediryl said, perfectly curved brows lifting. "Why, cousin! Have you taken an outworld friend? I would hardly have expected it. Between you and your brother, you were always the more conservative of the pair."

"We've been partners and friends for years now," Vasiht'h said, fighting irritation at her high-handed assumptions. "Many, many years."

"Oh, I've offended," she said, her facile manner dropping so abruptly he was taken aback. He barely had time to lean away as she dropped to a crouch before him, all her skirts whispering, and said, "Forgive me. And I did not greet you properly either . . . Aksivaht'h hold you in Her mind."

"Ah . . . and may Her thought of you be everlasting," Vasiht'h stammered.

"Is my apology acceptable?" she asked, a smile quirking her lips.

"At least you didn't accuse us of being lovers like the first group," Vasiht'h said, exasperation getting the better of him.

Sediryl laughed aloud. "A Glaseah? More fools they." She straightened, twitching her skirts into order with easy grace. "So, aunt. What are you scheming, then? Wanting to remind the inbred idiots they've betrothed Juzie to that the Galare are hardly the first to host an outworlder?"

"They're not?" Vasiht'h said, startled.

"Oh no," Sediryl said, seating herself across from a very stiff Jahir, who did not sit until she'd settled, and Jeasa after her. "No, Jisiensire has that honor. Sellelvi came to Fasianyl lo these many years ago. Rather too many, I think. The memory'll be lost soon enough, especially with that House so reclusive and its recent history so troubled."

"I didn't imagine you to be so easy with the goings-on here at home," Jeasa said hesitantly.

"I had my reasons to learn," Sediryl said, breezily. "But I fear I interrupted your explanation. Why do I find an offworlder here?"

"Because he is my son's friend," Jeasa said after a moment. "And . . ." She looked at Jahir, "I am tired of the insult given you. You are the heir to the Seni Galare, Jahir, and to pretend you do not have this relationship is a dishonor."

"Even if it jeopardizes the wedding?" Jahir asked.

"Perhaps the wedding is not worth it, if it cannot withstand a single outworlder," Jeasa said, and her silence then had something of resignation, and of sorrow, and Vasiht'h liked it not at all. Liked nothing of the entire situation, really, or the conversation, or anything implied by it.

Except possibly for Sediryl. She intrigued him, even though her existence betrayed yet another secret his partner had been withholding from him.

"Well!" Sediryl said. "I have only just arrived, and have not even been shown my rooms. I shall repair to them now, and recover from the long ride." When she rose, Jahir did also. "Good evening, my lady aunt, my lord heir." She grinned, all sharp angles and amusement, and curtseyed with exquisite grace to Jeasa before quitting the room.

Once she had gone, Jahir said, "We should do the same, I think."

"Will you be down to supper?" Jeasa asked, standing to take his hands again. Through the slight crack in the mindline, Vasiht'h felt the radiance of their quiet love for one another and let it soothe him.

"I think that may be . . . impolitic," Jahir said. "There will be time enough tomorrow to shock the guests, and with the wedding in the evening they will have less time to mull over the insult and perhaps decide it sufficient cause to depart. When is the reception?"

"In the mid-morning," Jeasa said. "The family still has an informal breakfast in the kitchen, if you're so inclined."

"We probably will be," Jahir said.

She nodded. "I'll have a tray sent up for you both for supper. If you need anything . . ."

"I'll ring a servant," Jahir said, and kissed the back of her hand. "Gentle night, lady mother."

"Thank you, love," she murmured.

⁂

Vasiht'h waited until they gained their rooms to fold his arms and look at his partner.

"Go ahead," Jahir said, tired.

"I'm not sure where to start," Vasiht'h said. "How about . . . just how royal are you? I thought you were joking when you told Nieve's girls you were a prince."

"Technically I'm not," Jahir said. "I said it to delight them, and because translating the titles into Universal is tiresome and inexact. And while I am related to the Queen, it's a distant kinship, and not one that would make me eligible to replace her.

If even a man could; by custom we have been matriarchal since Settlement, and by now custom looks like tradition, and precedent, and thus to us immutable."

"But you're close enough to the throne that your mother thinks it important to . . . make political deals to help cement the queen's policies?"

"My mother," Jahir said, sitting down and beginning to work his boots off, "is making political deals to help cement the queen's policies because without them, we will stagnate and die. We need the Alliance, arii. You have no idea how much."

The breath that came through the mindline had the damp coolth of a grave in winter. Vasiht'h shuddered, running a hand over his hair. "Right. So . . . your cousin . . . knew how to greet me?"

"She should, since she's been living on an Alliance starbase for years now," Jahir said, his voice gone neutral.

"She . . . what? She has?" Vasiht'h asked, startled. "I thought you all weren't much for wandering, that you were unusual?"

"I am," Jahir said. "She is also."

"She's so . . ." Vasiht'h trailed off, looking for a word. "She seems . . ."

"Bitter?" Jahir suggested.

"Angry," Vasiht'h said. "You said she had no lost love for your kind."

"She hasn't," Jahir said. "But she had other problems." At Vasiht'h's look, he said, "She loved a human man, and thought to wed him. Nothing about that situation went well."

Vasiht'h covered his face, slowly rubbed the bridge of his nose. "And this is the woman you're in love with."

Such abrupt tension through the mindline. It felt like being stabbed. "Ugh," Vasiht'h said. "Can you stop doing that? The slammed doors, the knives . . ."

"She's my *cousin*," Jahir said. "It's not done."

"What do you mean it's not done?" Vasiht'h said. "It's done all the time in the Alliance. Goddess, arii, the conservative homeworld Harat-Shar mate with their own siblings. It's what we have genetic engineers for—"

"*It's not done*," Jahir said, and the mindline exploded with nausea and self-loathing, with sickness and perversion and blooming red roses rotting and half-dead unborn children and Vasiht'h listed to one side, fighting the sudden urge to vomit and a revulsion so strong he almost lost his grip on reality.

Jahir's hands on his shoulders steadied him. "Sorry," the Eldritch whispered. "Arii. I'm sorry." When Vasiht'h could meet his eyes again, he said, one more time, "It's just . . . it's not done. Ever."

"Right," Vasiht'h said weakly.

"I'm going to have a bath," Jahir said after a long moment. "Do you want one also, or will you lie down until supper?"

He wasn't sure he'd be eating again . . . at all. Certainly not until tomorrow. "I think I'll lie down."

Jahir nodded. "There are more than enough cushions and blankets on the bed. Take as many as you need." His smile was wry. "No doubt the servants had no idea how to prepare a place for a Glaseah."

"I would have been surprised if they had," Vasiht'h said weakly.

He watched Jahir head to the bathing chamber. For a long time, he couldn't move. What had he gotten himself into, coming here? He had thought it would be a relief to finally know as much as he wanted about his partner, about the Eldritch, about the place and circumstances that had forged Jahir before Vasiht'h had met him. Not just a relief . . . but exciting. He'd always been pleased at having secured one of the rare Eldritch as a friend, at having merited that friendship. He had, occasionally, been proud of knowing as much as he did about one. It had felt good to be one of the few Alliance citizens who could speak knowledgeably about the reclusive species. He had earned no few admiring glances for it.

Looking back on it now, Vasiht'h could admit to perhaps having been unreasonably smug. Possibly a little vain . . . maybe a *lot* vain. He'd been so certain of himself.

Now, he was sitting in the middle of a possibly royal sitting room, with his hind end on a rug he probably couldn't have bought with a year's salary, wishing he was home, that he'd never come. Thinking that all that he'd guessed about Jahir's life before had been a fantasy. He'd created some fiction that Jahir had lived a life very like some wealthy person in the Alliance; more rural perhaps, a little quieter. But not . . . this entire alien philosophy, complete with hatred of strangers and contempt for change. Xenophobia had been, in his mind, more like mild distaste. A preference, like enjoying ice cream more than cake. Not the kind of thing that created political rifts so divisive they could induce civil war.

It felt very bad, being this wrong. He could not help but wonder how much trouble his wrongful assumptions would create.

Unsettled, Vasiht'h went to the bed chamber to begin plucking pillows off the monumental bed. The wedding was tomorrow. Surely he could get through one day here without too much more offense and go home, where it was safe. For them both.

——∞∞∞——

Vasiht'h woke from confused dreams of someone playing the lute to . . . the actual sound of lutesong, softened by the mindline's melancholy. He didn't rise immediately. The makeshift bed had been unexpectedly comfortable, and he had been tired enough from the long journey that he'd slept through dinner. Lifting his head, he glimpsed the bed: the blankets had been mussed, so at least his partner had slept also. But the lute . . .

He'd known Jahir could play piano, but it had somehow never occurred to him that his friend might know more than one instrument. How many skills had his much-older friend learned . . . and forgotten? Before Vasiht'h had ever been born?

His pelt twitched with unease. Something must have leaked through the line because the playing stopped. A few moments later, Jahir appeared at the door. "Ready for breakfast?"

Vasiht'h's stomach growled. He grimaced. "I guess that's

a yes. Do I have to wear something special? Do I have time to wash?"

"No and yes, respectively," Jahir said. "We eat breakfast informally . . . there will be no one there but close family. Actually, there might be no one there but us. It's not a sit-down affair, more of a catch-as-you-can."

"Oh," Vasiht'h said, relieved. "In that case . . . I'm all for it. Give me a minute and I'll be ready."

This time, less surprised by the wealth of the house, Vasiht'h noticed other things: its silence, for he heard almost nothing, no talk, no electronics, no music . . . nothing he might have expected. It was also empty, his partner's boots on the marble steps echoing as they went down the stairs. He saw no other people, despite the breadth of the halls and the many doors they passed. How many Eldritch lived in this palace? Where were they?

He was so perplexed that he didn't notice how long it took to reach the kitchen. He had been expecting a warm and cozy place, small, intimate. Like a kitchen in a book. Or barring that, something sterile and functional, like a kitchen in a restaurant. Naturally, they crossed a threshold into a vaulted chamber with enormous windows lining an entire wall, two separate niches for tables, both round, and a center island so long Vasiht'h could have fed his entire family at it.

The Eldritch cooks? Servants? However, were strangely comforting. They were not dressed in stunning silks and magnificent velvets, nor did they have a prince's ransom in jewels studding their hair like the garden-party attendees. They wore aprons over clothes with the simplicity of livery in blue and silver; the women had single braids down their backs or pinned into unadorned buns, and the men had their hair cropped or tied into short clubs. If they gave each other rather more space than Vasiht'h thought normal . . . well, they were touch-espers in a race that found that ability unpleasant.

Their entrance caused a great pause in the work. Through the mindline, the translation of Jahir's greeting was something like 'good morning' flavored with a downward grade that made

Vasiht'h feel as if he should brace his paws. While Jahir continued the exchange—something about how long it had been since
his last visit and other niceties—Vasiht'h poked the mindline
until he got some reason for the feeling: something about proper
polite speech to servants being different than to other peers
in the nobility. He made a face, glad he didn't have to learn the
language.

"So, ready for breakfast?" Jahir said in Universal, perching
on a stool at the end of the island.

"Absolutely," Vasiht'h said. He watched the bustle. "So these
are . . . um . . . employees?"

"Family retainers," Jahir said. "Most of them have been
working for us for generations."

"Generations!"

"It is good work," Jahir said, "being household staff. If you
can secure such a position, you can expect your son or daughter
to inherit it, and so on. Your family will have food and shelter
and a stipend and the assurance of that continuing for as long as
you and your descendants provide good service."

Vasiht'h stared at the basket of rolls a young girl placed in
front of them with a shy smile. "I . . . can't imagine it."

"Our economy is . . . odd in compare to the Alliance usual,"
Jahir said, with such irony Vasiht'h tasted metal salts in his
mouth. He licked his teeth and reached for a roll.

"What is the day going to be like then?" Vasiht'h said, to
change the subject and defuse the potential for more bad tastes.
"I mean, schedule-wise. I don't know anything about Eldritch
weddings." He made a face. "I don't even know much about Glaseahn weddings, to be honest. Except that everyone wears bells."

"Bells?" Jahir said, amused.

"Something about honoring the Goddess and blessing the
union with fertility and happiness," Vasiht'h said.

One of the cooks arrived, setting a platter in arm's reach:
strips of meat fragrant with strange spices wound around thin
yellow sticks and decorated with citrus slices, a selection of other
mysterious fruits: slices of pale peach melons and berries of

various sizes and colors. More of the rolls with a plate of white butter, sweating in the kitchen's warmth. The young girl brought a tea pot and a pitcher of ice water.

"Heavy for breakfast," Vasiht'h said, trying one of the meat slices. It was a peculiar experience: his palate insisted he had never had anything like it before while the mindline insisted it was familiar and comfortable. "I would have thought you sub-sisted on flowers and moonbeams, the way everyone around here looks."

"Breakfast is the heavy meal of the day for the servants," Jahir said. "And we are eating in the kitchen. The heavy meal of the day for us is usually lunch. And the physique has less to do with diet and more to do with the gravity here, and the fact that if you do not ride here, you walk." He leaned back as he but-tered a roll, one elbow on the island. "So, the wedding. In a few hours there will be a reception for the wedding party and atten-dants—the bride and groom will be absent, by custom. Everyone will retire after that to eat lunch and then to dress and prepare for the ceremony, which is at dusk. The ceremony lasts an hour, and then there is another reception, which the bride and groom attend, and everyone else who's come. That lasts until very late at night, unless there is significant acrimony."

"And all I have to do is . . ."

"Mingle at the party and watch the ceremony," Jahir said. "And then we can head home."

"Sounds do-able," Vasiht'h said, and dug into breakfast. He couldn't tell if he liked it because it was good or if he liked it because Jahir did, but he was willing to work with either.

∞

His willingness evaporated the moment he espied the great hall through the broad arched doorway later that morning; if the mirrors and chandeliers were not dazzling enough, the number of Eldritch would have sufficed. Their identical skin and hair color made them appear distressingly like multiples of a similar doll, and their sumptuous raiment put them far above someone of his rather unremarkable provenance. He marveled that just looking at them he could feel the aura of contempt and privilege they exuded; that he could tell, just by that glimpse, that he wouldn't be welcome.

At the dismay that flooded the mindline, Jahir went to a knee before him, resting his gloved hands on Vasiht'h's shoulders. In a way, that made it worse: he'd never seen his partner dressed as a . . . well, a native. The court coat Jahir wore was velvet, dyed a powder-blue at the flared skirt that gradually darkened to sapphire at the collar, no doubt to set off the white cravat with its unicorn pin. There were strands of opals and sapphires in slim silver chains worked into tiny braids in Jahir's hair, and Vasiht'h had no doubt they were real. He even had a sword, complete with decorative scabbard; the coat had some kind of slit to permit it. The Eldritch looked like something out of a storybook, and seeing the friend Vasiht'h had worked alongside for years looking so . . . alien . . . was uncomfortably like waking up next to a stranger.

"You need not do this," Jahir murmured, his voice mingling with the hum of conversation from the room. Through the mindline, Vasiht'h felt a softness, like a blanket. "I do not expect it of you."

"Will . . . I be able to talk with anyone?" Vasiht'h asked. He'd been invited; it seemed rude to not make an appearance. "I mean, do they understand Universal?"

"Some of them," Jahir said. "It is more likely true of my family. They'll be the ones with the unicorn device on them somewhere, as a brooch or a necklace, and many of them will have blue or silver on them. The visiting family's colors are green and electrum, and their device is a centicore . . . like a hooved lion."

"I'll try it," Vasiht'h said before he could lose his nerve. "But if it gets too hard . . ."

"By all means," Jahir said. "I will have to stay—that is my duty as the son of the house. But if you become uncomfortable, you needn't."

"All right," Vasiht'h said, squaring his shoulders. He drew in a breath. "Let's go."

Jahir nodded and rose smoothly. Together they walked just within the threshold where the Eldritch stopped; Vasiht'h did also, perplexed. And then a man in the house's livery announced them, and mangled his name in the process.

All conversation ceased.

/Oh, Goddess,/ Vasiht'h whispered.

/Strength, arii,/ Jahir murmured back, and waited a heartbeat so the room could look its fill before striding into it. Vasiht'h hurried after him, tucking his wings close against his back and trying not to notice the stares and the hissing whispers he couldn't understand. He found himself regretting his vest: it was his nicest, a dark red embroidered with birds and stylized clouds edging the bottom all the way to the back where the clouds entwined in an abstract representation of Aksivaht'h's breath. But now that he was surrounded by these incredibly over-dressed people, he suddenly wished he had used the more formal sari he'd been reserving for the ceremony itself.

"Hello, my son," Jeasa said, joining them. She spoke in Universal, but Vasiht'h noted she didn't take Jahir's hands. Perhaps such a gesture was too intimate—or outré—for the company they were in. "Did you pass the night well?"

"Very," Jahir said.

"And you?" Jeasa asked Vasiht'h, smiling.

"Ah . . . well enough, thank you," Vasiht'h said. "We did a little improvising for a bed."

"Oh, I am glad," she said. "And thank you for joining us. I know it's difficult when you don't speak the language."

Relaxing a little, Vasiht'h said, "Ah, it's my pleasure, ma'am."

"And what," a voice behind them said, the translated words echoing down the mindline tinged with ice and contempt so thick it dripped acid, "is this? I thought this was a civilized gathering."

Jeasa looked over Vasiht'h's head and answered, and Jahir's translation of her voice gave it a quality that felt like winter air, biting the inside of his nose. "This is my son's companion, Carisil."

"What is it?" the woman said, sweeping in front of them

to look. She was taller than Jeasa, with a face of severe, and—
Vasiht'h thought—unfair beauty. She was gowned in peacock
green, and there was so much fabric in her skirt that he could
only wonder how much it had cost just to swathe the woman's
narrow hips. "A pet of some kind?"

Jeasa began with some heat, "That is no pet—"

Jahir held up a hand, and his words tasted like steel under
Vasiht'h's tongue, and the feel of it was so alien that it took him
a moment to realize his friend was being condescending. Was
capable of condescension, something Vasiht'h had never in his
life heard from him. "Gently, mother. I am certain it is ignorance,
no more. After all, not all families have access to the education
we do, coming as it does at such great expense over the royal
Wellfeed."

"We have the means," the woman sniffed. "We merely do not
spend it on such . . . things." She looked at Vasiht'h with nar-
rowed eyes.

"I'm glad the Alliance was spared," Vasiht'h muttered.

The woman gasped. "Why, it—"

"—speaks, I know," Vasiht'h said, answering her Eldritch
words in Universal. He sighed and folded his arms. "So shocking."

"This is the mother of the groom," Jahir said in like tongue,
his voice careless but the mindline rich with contempt.

"Really," the woman was saying to Jeasa, the words lagging
as Jahir's attention did, "there is no call for a . . . display . . . of
this . . . vulgarity. This is a solemn occasion."

"I will not hear one of my guests spoken of in this way," Jeasa
answered, voice growing stern.

"First you invite a known reprobate to the ceremony, knowing
what a bad example she would be to a virgin bride," the woman
replied. "Now this? Is there no end to the . . . eccentricity . . . of
your household?"

/Am I really going to cause this much trouble?/ Vasiht'h asked,
appalled at how quickly the situation was spiraling out of control.

Jahir hesitated before answering. */Your presence here could be
construed as . . . unusual./*

/How *unusual?*/ Vasiht'h asked, acidly.

/*You might be the first alien these people have ever seen,*/ Jahir answered, wry like sour oranges.

Vasiht'h's claws flexed, nearly visible. He glanced around the party; the conversation had resumed, but only in quick whispers. Everyone was either staring at them, or standing in a way that they could stare without being obvious. *This was a bad idea. Me even coming was a bad idea.*/

/*Arii—*/

/*No arguing,*/ Vasiht'h said, torn between disgust and humiliation, and not understanding either. Fine state for a therapist, he thought to himself, and it was one of the first times he could remember that he actively blocked a thought from his friend.

And that scared him.

/*I'm leaving,*/ he said curtly, his mind-voice edged.

/*All right,*/ Jahir said. No anger, no surprise. Somehow, the blanket-soft understanding made it worse. Vasiht'h turned his back on all of them and marched out, his spine stiff from the tail all the way up to the nape of his neck. And he kept marching all the way into the halls, where he found himself shaking. He squelched the mindline until it was nothing but a murmur in the back of his head and set off, wondering where he would go to escape an entire planetful of Eldritch, when he didn't even know how to get out of the house.

Angry, he stopped in front of one of the house's servants. "Where's the exit?" he asked boldly, expecting nothing.

So he was startled when the man answered, in accented but polite Universal, "Continue down this hall, please, and follow the corridors that broaden."

This he did, then, quicker and quicker until he found he was almost running when he reached the foyer, and plunged outside into the light. He didn't stop moving either, until he was part of the way up the road. Stopping to look back over his shoulder, he found the manor exactly as it should have been; not on fire, not exploding, not doing any of the things he felt it should be to reflect how disordered his emotional state was. It remained, implacable, expensive, too large, like an indictment of him for being content with normal things, mundane things like a little apartment, a quiet practice . . . and an alien friend.

Vasiht'h sighed, shoulders drooping. He didn't want to go back. But going forward—he looked that way.

. . . and saw, unexpectedly, a child on a pony and a woman strolling alongside with a parasol. The woman, he saw when she turned her face to answer a question, was Sediryl.

Why not, he thought. *At least she knows a language I can speak.* So he trotted toward them, and when he was close enough, called, "Is this . . . um . . . walking party open?"

Sediryl and the child both looked back at him.

The child squealed. "A Glaseah a Glaseah a real Glaseah!"

Sediryl laughed. "I think that's a 'yes you can join us'," she said. "Come along, arii. Us strangefolk need to stick together, mm?"

Surprised by the child's reaction, Vasiht'h joined them and glanced at her. She was a cute thing; somehow he'd thought Eldritch children would look like their parents, born snooty and perfect. But she had a snub nose and a friendly smile and eyes too large for the face she was still growing into, and while she wore finery that Vasiht'h found appallingly expensive to be subjected to a bareback pony-ride, she was already grubby in a way that was charmingly normal for a little girl.

"You speak Universal?" he asked her cautiously.

"Yes," she answered, lifting her chin. "I'm a Galare. We *all* speak Universal."

"I see," Vasiht'h murmured.

"This," Sediryl said, strolling up to flank him on the other side, "is Juzie, the bride."

"The . . . bride?" Vasiht'h said. "Uh . . . Eldritch . . . bodies . . . age differently? Than humanoid?"

"Oh, no," Sediryl said cheerfully, twirling the parasol and kicking up the hem of her skirt as she walked. "She's as young as she looks. Horrifying, isn't it?"

"Mother and Aunt said I'm not to do anything I don't want to do until I feel old enough," the girl added.

For a moment, Vasiht'h couldn't speak. He wanted to press his hands to his head to keep it from throbbing, but didn't want to offend either of them. "So . . . wait. If you're the bride, where are you going?"

"The wedding's not for hours!" the girl said. "I want to go to the commons to buy some candy. While I'm still single."

"And she needed a chaperone, of course," Sediryl said.

The girl giggled. "Luckily no one saw us leave, or they would have had fits."

"Because . . . you're not supposed to be going?" Vasiht'h guessed.

"Because I'm a completely unsuitable guardian," Sediryl said. "And there's not a soul among our guests who doesn't know that." She grinned, all teeth. "My behavior was so absolutely *scandalous* that I have been the talk of the courts for years."

"And also because I really shouldn't be going," Juzie agreed.

"So . . . you're . . . going somewhere you shouldn't, with someone you shouldn't be with, and no one saw you leave," Vasiht'h said.

"Yes," the girl said, pleased. "I think it's a fine adventure. Cousin Sediryl was just telling me that it's customary for people who are about to get married to do one wild thing before they settle down. It's called a bachelorette event."

Vasiht'h's body started shaking. He wasn't sure if it was laughter or some kind of mental breakdown. When he had control over himself again, he said to Sediryl, "You really are a bad influence."

"If my entire society is going to condemn me as a fallen woman for a single mistake," Sediryl said, "I might as well revel in the role." She grinned. "So, want to go buy some candy?"

"Oh yes, please!" the girl said. "Come with us? I've never seen a real outworlder before! You're so pretty!"

Vasiht'h laughed, maybe with a little more exhaustion than he liked. But at least he was laughing. "Sure. I'd like to see what Eldritch candy is like."

"Excellent," Sediryl said. "Off we go, then."

"Can you fly?" Juzie asked eagerly. "The wings, do they work? Why do you have feathers for ears? How do you sleep? Can you run faster than a horse?"

"Slow down!" Vasiht'h said, holding up his hands. "One question at a time!"

The girl bounced on her pony. "Are you a girl Glaseah or a boy? I can't tell."

At Vasiht'h's expression, Sediryl laughed. "It's going to be an interesting walk."

—⦵—

It was, in fact, an interesting walk. Juzie's questions were born of an unquenchable enthusiasm; remembering Jeasa's intention to intrigue the groom, Vasiht'h couldn't help but think the plan had a good chance of success. There was not a drop of contempt in Juzie, who was fascinated by him and insatiably curious. He answered all the questions he could as they walked down the dusty road, on matters ranging from anatomy to culture to language. The girl was smart as well as good-natured, and he enjoyed her company.

She did eventually run out of questions, however . . . either that, or she needed time to assimilate his answers. Probably the latter, knowing children; in his experience, any pause in questioning was just that: a pause. As the girl rode her pony beneath the leaf-shaped shadows, Vasiht'h dropped back to look around. The forest on either side of the road was without underbrush, unlike the woods where he was from which were more like jungles. His inefficient ears did not bring him much more than the sound of the pony's hooves and the wind through the boughs, but his more sensitive nose whispered glad intimations of spring, new flowers, piquant and unknown to him.

"Pretty world, isn't it?" Sediryl said, joining him. "A pity it's full of Eldritch."

Startled, Vasiht'h burst out laughing and covered his mouth, appalled.

Sediryl chuckled, twirling her parasol again. "Oh, don't bother. They're horrid, we both know it."

"So why did you come, if you hate them so much?" Vasiht'h asked, glancing up at her.

"I don't hate *all* of them," Sediryl said. "Just almost all of them. And I came to remind myself of why I left." She grinned without humor. "It took a few minutes of being in their company. I could leave now."

"But you haven't," Vasiht'h said.

"Well . . . no." She smiled a little, lowering her brilliant, cutting eyes, her lashes casting shadows on her cheeks. "I have my reasons."

Vasiht'h began to wonder how many of those reasons had to do with his partner. Either that, he thought ruefully, or Sediryl was nourishing thoughts of disrupting the wedding in some cataclysmic fashion. "Jahir tells me you live off-world?"

"On a starbase," she said, recovering her more glib manner. "Did he tell you about my lovers, then?"

"Ah . . ."

"I've had several," she said. "You know, perfectly scandalous." She leaned toward him, eyes wide. "I'm not a *virgin* anymore."

"I suppose that's important here?" Vasiht'h proffered.

She laughed. "Oh, poor Glaseah. And you're attached at the hip to Jahir? You have no idea what you're in for. Procreation here, lines of descent, purity of bloodline . . . all very important. Of paramount importance." She grinned again, like a hunting animal. "He hasn't been teaching you the language, I assume, what with the Veil."

"Right," Vasiht'h said.

"Then I'll teach you your first profanity," Sediryl said with relish. "Repeat after me: *elorim*."

"*ELORIM*," Juzie shouted.

"Hush you," Sediryl called. "Listen all you want, but never admit to eavesdropping on the conversation of your elders. That'll make them stop talking around you."

"Yes, cousin," Juzie said with a giggle.

"And what . . . exactly . . . does *elorim* mean?" Vasiht'h asked, cautious.

"It's what we call someone so inbred he's a danger to everyone around him," Sediryl said. "If you want, you can also call someone a *linith*—that's a bastard, and nearly as bad. People have died in duels over being called those names." Her smile relaxed. "So I lost my virginity to a human, who didn't marry me, and this makes me used goods. And then I took a woman lover, and that was just as bad—one does not dally with one's sex here, you understand. Very, very bad. And now I am unrepentantly living on my own in alien space, something scandalous enough for a man, but absolutely unheard of in a woman. I will never fit back into Eldritch society as it stands. Your partner . . . he'll come back and be head of the Seni Galare one day, as heir; not even having you for a companion will save him from that, given his breeding. But there will never be a place again for me here. So I come back. To remember that I don't miss it."

"Do you?" Vasiht'h asked.

With unwonted gravity, Sediryl said, "No." And with a sigh, with more melancholy. "No. You'll see soon enough."

That seemed ominous. Vasiht'h was debating whether to ask for details when the girl cried out, "We made it!"

The forest petered out on either side of the road, leaving it to wander down through . . . what could charitably be called a shanty town. He counted twenty ramshackle buildings and a few hovels bordering the road, and the air of decrepitude and disrepair was shocking.

"What is *that*?" Vasiht'h asked.

"That is the town nearest to the Galare manor," Sediryl said, stopping beside him. Before them, Juzie had urged her pony into a canter down into the commons.

"This is a *town*?" Vasiht'h asked, mouth agape and feathered ears splayed.

"This is a big town," Sediryl corrected. "There are a few more down the road, but there will only be a handful of people left in them."

"But what *happened*?" Vasiht'h asked, turning to her.

"*Elorim*," Sediryl said. "Generations and generations of people turning up their noses at hard work, decent people, and the help of the outworlders . . . or even their neighbors. Generations of people elevated to the nobility so they wouldn't have to lift a finger to do anything more difficult than call for another cup of wine, or plan another party." She raised her head, pointing toward the commons with her chin. "When too many things break here, the inhabitants will move down the road to the next place where things still work. They say the town 'died'. Because no one knows how to maintain anything anymore."

"But . . . the estate . . . the beautiful house . . ."

"Look at it more closely when you get back," Sediryl said. "Everything there is old, Vasiht'h-alet. It's old because no one knows how to make things like that anymore. Or to repair them when they start to fail. All those gorgeous tapestries, the woodwork, the jewelry, the instruments . . . all of it a dwindling or lost art." She smiled lopsidedly. "We're lucky the house servants remember how to keep gardens and kill chickens, or there'd be no food, and in a few decades, no Eldritch at all."

Vasiht'h's haunches gave out, dropping him to a seat in the dust. "Then this wedding . . ."

". . . is one of my House's attempts at helping revive an interest in the outworld, in the hopes that maybe one day we'll let you people in to fix things before it's too late."

"And that's why I'm here," Vasiht'h said, heart beating too fast. "Because I represent a chance for survival."

"One that my aunt couldn't help but reach out to, despite knowing how much it would offend the groom's family," Sediryl said, resting the point of her parasol on the ground and leaning forward on the handle. "She doesn't have the patience the Queen does." She made a face. "Though Liolesa's playing a game so long we might all be dead before it comes to fruition. I wish she'd just *DO* something."

"Jahir's mother said just doing something might inspire a civil war," Vasiht'h said, still shocked.

"Yes," Sediryl said. "But a civil war might get rid of all the dead weight." She grinned, with teeth. "Bring in some of the Alliance's racial genetic engineers and the rest of us will take care of the future."

"Goddess," Vasiht'h whispered, feeling cold all over. "What have I gotten involved in?"

"Nothing less than the life or death struggle of an entire race," Sediryl said, lifting her parasol back to her shoulder. "Exciting isn't it?"

Vasiht'h stared at her, horrified. She met his expression with a grin and said, "The candy awaits." And strolled down the road after Juzie.

Vasiht'h did not enter the dilapidated building where Juzie and Sediryl were buying their sweets. He had initially feared the possibility of being seen, but there was no one on the street, and when he glanced at the windows, most of them had drawn curtains, or looked like dark sockets in the skulls of their facades, without anyone behind them to give them life.

He found it ironic that standing in the middle of a nearly empty town, he felt more painfully exposed than he had in a room full of sneering Eldritch. Exposed . . . and somehow endangered. He rubbed his arms against the grain of the fur, trying to generate some warmth to counter the chill in his joints, one he knew very well had nothing to do with the weather.

Not long after, Sediryl exited the building with the girl at her heels. Both of them had little bags, and the girl was sucking on some kind of golden ball.

"Want some?" Juzie said, offering a piece to Vasiht'h.

"It's pynade," Sediryl added. "Nuts, honey and spices."

"No thank you," Vasiht'h said mechanically. "Hard candy hurts my teeth."

Sediryl took Juzie's bag as the girl pulled herself back onto her pony's back. "I see . . . only the softest cakes for our alien, eh?" Before Vasiht'h could answer, she handed him a little candy shaped like a swan. "Here. Eldritch marzipan. It's chewy, not hard."

"Thank you," Vasiht'h said, and followed the two of them back up the road. He glanced over his shoulder at the town, then nibbled on the swan. He was hungry. It seemed like hours since they'd left, though he had no idea how to tell the local time. The light was different . . . his shadow longer. He frowned at it as it rippled over the uneven road. "Are we going to be back in time?"

"We'll be fine," Sediryl said, biting off the head of her marzipan swan.

There didn't seem any argument with that. The candy kept Juzie occupied, and Sediryl had no more poisonous (or terrifying) commentary to share, so Vasiht'h kept pace with the pony, accepted a sugared leaf or nut from Sediryl when the woman offered one, and tried to work through his feelings . . . entirely without success. He thought about tapping the mindline, but he was beginning to feel guilty for abandoning Jahir and then going quiet on him. He didn't look forward to making explanations for his unusual behavior. He wouldn't deny he had his passionate moments; his life with Jahir had demonstrated that often enough. But he didn't usually fluster this easily. Surely, though, he could be excused for having a fit when confronted with the possible extinction of an entire race. One that hated him. He sighed and licked sugar off his fingertips, and tried to concentrate on the feel of the breeze on his back and the smell of flowers in his nose. If the world was going topsy-turvy, at least it was beautiful.

Perhaps Sediryl was reading his mind, for she murmured, looking around, "Oh, the things I could do with this place if given the chance. Lying so fallow, completely undeveloped . . ." At his look, she said, "I'm a botanist."

"A . . . a botanist?" Vasiht'h asked, startled.

"Of course," she said. "Normal people have jobs." She smiled lopsidedly. "I work in agronomy in the starbase's agriculture sphere. I love my job. One of the other reasons I don't live here. Women's job opportunities here are limited to 'menial', 'lady's maid' and 'broodmare'. If you can't get 'head of household' or 'queen,' that is."

"A botanist," Vasiht'h repeated, trying to imagine a farmer's jumpsuit on the urbane, lithe young woman pacing him in her russet-colored gown with its pounds of ribbon and silk trim and gossamer undergown and . . . goddess only knew what other absurdities were required to keep such vast dresses afloat.

Sediryl grinned at him slyly over her latest marzipan fancy, some kind of leaping fish, and nipped off its fin. And suddenly he could see it: ears of wheat braided into her hair and dirt smudged on her pale cheeks.

"I want to have a job one day," Juzie said.

"Maybe you will, cousin," Sediryl said lazily. "You've got a long life ahead of you."

"And I won't let my husband stop me," Juzie said, lifting her chin. "I'm a *Galare*. I've got royal blood."

"Just so, sweetings," Sediryl said with a grin.

The poor boy, Vasiht'h thought. He hardly knew what he was in for. Vasiht'h had some sympathy there.

∞

It was late afternoon when they finally gained the path to the manor, but neither Juzie nor Sediryl seemed worried, so Vasiht'h kept close to them and hoped their little indiscretion had gone unnoticed. He'd go inside and scrub the dust off his feet and belly and meet Jahir in time for the ceremony and all would be, if not well, then at least as close to normal as could be hoped for. As they walked toward the house, Vasiht'h glanced to either side, into the gardens and toward the fountains, hoping not to be seen.

By the time they'd gotten most of the way down the path, Vasiht'h was beginning to be concerned that there was no one to see them.

"Where is everyone?" he said to Sediryl.

"Oh, inside preparing, no doubt," Sediryl said. She motioned to her bodice. "Do you know how long it takes Eldritch to dress in these get-ups? It requires servants. And that's nothing to the hair. Braiding a dragon's hoard onto your head takes time. Plus, no showers, you know. Baths are leisurely affairs."

"Right," Vasiht'h said, his shoulders relaxing a little.

And then they broke from the path and the doors to the manor spilled a river of Eldritch . . . onto the steps, onto the packed earth before them, more and more of them until Vasiht'h backed away and almost into the pony, which responded with a bored sidestep.

At the top of the stairs, nearest the door, were Jahir and his mother . . . and the groom's mother, and a man Vasiht'h assumed to be his father, and an array of relatives with similar faces. The expressions on those faces were not heartening.

/Um, Jahir?/ Vasiht'h managed weakly. /Am I in trouble?/

Jahir's face was a mask, but a sense of resignation seeped into the mindline as it opened more fully, bringing with it foreboding, like the scent of rotting fruit. /Let me guess. My cousin's idea./

/Yesssss . . ./

"What is this!" the groom's mother hissed, the translation throwing off red flashes of light in the mindline. "What have you done! The bride is supposed to remain in the company of family before the wedding!"

"I am family," Sediryl said dryly, the words almost a drawl when translated.

"That woman is an inappropriate role model!" the woman exclaimed. "She is a—"

"—watch your next word carefully, madam," Jahir said, all cold steel.

"—a woman of uncertain morals!" the woman finished.

"But still family," Sediryl said cheerily, twirling her parasol again.

"She is correct," Jeasa said, voice quiet. "One can fault her for her morals, Carisil, but no rule was broken. Juzie was with family."

"THAT," the woman said, pointing at Vasiht'h. "is NOT family. That is an alien. Goddess knows what ideas it has put in the bride's head."

"She has no idea who the dangerous one is here," Sediryl said sotto voce, in Universal, to Vasiht'h.

"This is not funny!" Vasiht'h whispered back, all his fur on end.

"Well?" Carisil asked, with a note of triumph in her voice that Vasiht'h could hear even without the translation. "I am correct, am I not? You have permitted someone into the bride's presence who is not family before the ceremony."

"The outworlder guest is extended the courtesies of the family they're visiting," Jeasa began, her voice colored all over with dismay.

"—but that doesn't make them true family!" the groom's mother said.

"No," Sediryl said, interrupting them. "But there is a way for outworlders to be *made* true-family."

Complete silence. Everyone stared at her. She smiled, eyes half-lidded, and rested the parasol on her shoulder.

"Sediryl?" Jeasa said. "You speak truly?"

"Jisiensire was not only the first to host an outworlder," Sediryl said. "It was also the first House to welcome an outworlder into its ranks. A ritual was created especially for that purpose. It can be done."

"And do you know how it may be done?" Jeasa asked.

"I do," Sediryl said smugly.

Another long pause. One by one, the Eldritch's gazes moved to Vasiht'h, who tried not to tremble under their pressure. The mindline remained quiet in the aftermath of the colored translations, leaving him alone to make his choice. He lifted his head and said, very clearly, "Tell them I'll do it. Right now."

Sediryl grinned at him and obliged, and the crowd erupted into noise: objections, speculation, cheers, confusion. Amid it all, someone came for Juzie and Sediryl shepherded Vasiht'h up the steps to where Jeasa was standing beside the groom's mother.

"We will want to witness," Carisil said stiffly.

"Of course," Sediryl said. "The ceremony requires it." And

with a motion, whisked them all into the hall before the throng could follow.

To Sediryl as they strode on, Jeasa said, "You know what you're doing, I hope, my niece."

"Absolutely," Sediryl said. "It's a real ceremony. I had reasons of my own to research it." Her smile grew thinner. "We'll need the evening. If you can use your Alliance-borrowed technology, Aunt, you can get a copy of how it proceeds from the capital . . . the Queen created the rite with the help of the Church, and there's a copy of it in her datastore."

Jeasa stared at her. "Only the heads of the Galare families are supposed to know about that datastore."

Sediryl snorted. "If she'd wanted to keep everyone else out of it, she should have protected it better. Anyone with basic computer knowledge could find it."

Behind them, Jahir said quietly, "That's probably the point."

Both women glanced back at him.

"The Eldritch who want nothing to do with the Alliance would hardly know how to use a computer," Jahir said. "So she left it open for the ones who cared enough to do so, for their use."

"Convoluted but clever," Sediryl said. "Sounds like her."

"In here," Jeasa said, opening the door into the same salon she'd greeted them in the first day. "I shall check the computer and come right back."

"I'll go with you, show you where to find it," Sediryl said.

Which left Vasiht'h alone with his partner for the first time since mid-morning . . . when he'd shut the mindline down to its lowest trickle. He looked at Jahir, chagrined. "I'm sorry about earlier."

"I am the one who must beg your pardon," Jahir said, the words sagging in the mindline, as if exhausted. He sat on a chair and leaned forward, propping his elbows on his knees and hanging his hands between them, fingers entwined. It relaxed Vasiht'h, to see it . . . they had been compensating for their differences in height for so long that the move to put their heads on the same level felt reassuringly normal. He had not damaged the relationship, after all . . . not too much, anyway.

"I should have known this would become complicated," Jahir finished. "I was so intent on having something—someone—sane and familiar at my side that I dragged you here, knowing that it would certainly become uncomfortable for you."

"Well, that's done already," Vasiht'h said. "And I can't blame you. I decided to come myself . . . I have myself to blame for that, even if—" holding up a hand to forestall Jahir's protest, a pressure building in the mindline, "—I didn't fully understand what I was getting into." Goddess, how he hadn't understood what he was getting into! "But arii, there's a far more important thing to discuss now."

"Which is?" Jahir asked, eyes resting on Vasiht'h's.

"Do you *want* me to be part of your family?" Vasiht'h asked, sheepish. "I said yes because . . . I mean, I had to, or your mother's plan would have exploded. Wouldn't it have?"

"Yes," Jahir admitted. "They seek reasons to call it off, but they feel they must be able to claim they were in the right to do so. They must have a legitimate cause."

"So I said 'yes.' Before I asked you. But I should have asked," Vasiht'h said, shoulders slumping. "I don't want to force my way in to your life like this. Your life *here*, which is not at all the same as the life we made together somewhere else."

Jahir's smile was gentle, a little sad. "I think the more pertinent question is whether *you* want to become family to *me*, with all that entails. I would think, anyway. Now that you understand more fully just what a tangle you will be entering into at my side."

Vasiht'h opened his mouth to say 'of course I do' and then closed it with a click. He frowned, thinking of the mess he would be inheriting—would feel obliged to help with, the way he would with his own people. Family was a sacred obligation, even among Glaseah with their artificial creation of it . . . perhaps because of the artificial creation of it. It was the more precious because it had to be worked for so hard, in defiance of biology. And the entire Eldritch species was, if Jahir, Sediryl and the evidence of his own eyes were to be believed, obnoxious, xenophobic . . . and in desperate trouble. It would be like marrying into a family deep in debt and peopled entirely by the mentally and physically ill.

And yet, there were the Jeasas. And the Juzies. And even the Sediryls . . .

. . . and particularly the Jahirs.

"I wouldn't want to be a part of any Eldritch's family," Vasiht'h said. "But I would like to be part of yours."

Jahir held out a hand to him and he took it. The mindline deepened, smoothed out, filled with a wordless reassurance. Vasiht'h sighed, relieved.

———

"*No*," Jahir said, the word bulkhead-hard in the mindline, with all its menacing connotations of the lethal vacuum behind it. "No, this is absolutely intolerable."

"It's how the rite is done," Sediryl insisted.

"You cannot fling a drug at a completely different species and expect it to work," Jahir said, louring over the table at her. "Harat-Shar are *not* Glaseah. They are *emphatically* not Glaseah. They are not even the same generation of Pelted."

"But the Glaseah were engineered by them," Sediryl said. "It's probably a similar design, biologically."

"Sediryl! Don't play the idiot with me!" Jahir exclaimed. "You better than anyone else here know the volatility of plant chemistries!"

"And that's all I do," she answered. "I don't know a thing about how they interact with people medically. But presumably the person who designed the whole thing did know, because it worked. The rite requires an altered state of consciousness, Jahir. *Requires* it, so that the outworlder's mind can be examined. Would you prefer one of us knock him on the head?"

"A concussion would be safer than to him administering a potentially toxic preparation!" Jahir said.

Observing the argument, the groom's mother said, "Does this mean the rite is called off?"

Jahir glared at her. Sediryl, whose back was to the woman,

rolled her eyes.

Vasiht'h had been watching the entire debate, which had erupted the moment the document—a conveniently appearing one that even looked handwritten—had been brought into the room with the groom's family. They had insisted on their inclusion in the discussion, and since the point of undergoing the rite was to appease them, Vasiht'h hadn't objected. He hadn't objected to anything yet, actually, though the description of every part of the rite so far had proved daunting.

But then, he hadn't needed to object; Jahir had been his ardent protector through the entirety of the discussion, speaking so rapidly the translation lag was distinct. He'd begun arguing when the aim of the rite had been made clear: to allow the Eldritch participants a chance to evaluate the outworlder mentally and see how well he conformed to the ideals of trustworthiness, integrity, honor, and magnanimity. And naturally, the eternally-fearful Eldritch required the potentially dangerous outworlder in question to be helpless and open to suggestion, which entailed the ingestion of a drug.

"We can't ask him to risk his life for this," Jahir said, looking at his mother, speaking in pointed Universal. The scorn and anger in his voice was so naked Vasiht'h wondered how it was affecting their witnesses. "To placate these people! If they are so desperate not to marry into our House—our *royal* House!—let them find some other child-bride for their useless son!"

Jeasa looked at Vasiht'h, and in her eyes, he saw sorrow and compassion and resignation intermingled, an expression that softened her face and made her look old. "You're right," she said at last. She turned to Carisil.

"I'll do it," Vasiht'h interrupted, before she could speak.

"Arii!" Jahir said, aghast. "You can't be serious. *There's no medicine on this world worth speaking of.* If you have a reaction to the drug, the limits of what they can do for you is give you an emetic and hope you vomit it up in time!"

Vasiht'h nodded at Sediryl. "She said Sellelvi took it, and she's probably not wrong about the Glaseah sharing a lot physiologically with the first and second generation Pelted."

"It probably worked on Sellelvi *because* it was toxic," Jahir said. "If I had a lab, if I had a chemical analyzer, if I had any useful tool at all! I could probably make a guess as to what it would do to you—"

"But you don't," Vasiht'h said, feeling an unnatural calm. "And this has to be done." He tipped his chin at the groom's family. "Tell them we'll do it now, so that I have time to keep the entire vigil before the night ends, as required."

Jahir stared at him. The mindline ached as he said, /I don't want you to die./

Vasiht'h met his eyes. /But I will. Will it matter if it's now or in seventy years? Compared to your lifetime?/

Jahir's pupils dilated abruptly and he took one step back, as if from a blow.

"We're wasting time," Vasiht'h said to Sediryl. "Let's get it over with." Before, he thought, he lost his nerve.

It was a lonely thought, with only himself to hear it. The mindline was empty, without even a hiss to suggest it remained.

———∞∞∞———

So it was Jeasa who led him to the family chapel, down stone halls that echoed with the sound of her slippers, much lighter tones than those produced by the weight of Jahir's boots. He found he missed them, that their lack at his side made his fur fluff up in unease.

"Vasiht'h," she said, and her attempt at his name was credible, "are you certain about this?"

"Ma'am," Vasiht'h said, "I am not. But . . ."

He trailed off, wondering why he was so resolved on going through with it, and not precisely knowing. He found the mystery of his own motivations uncomfortable. All he knew was that with every passing moment, he felt it more urgently: not to back down in front of these people, and not to abandon them.

"But," he finished, "I'm going to do it anyway."

"My son," she said quietly, "is rotted through with fear for you."

That was a strange enough statement that Vasiht'h wondered if it was lifted directly from some Eldritch idiom. He glanced at her. "When this is over, we'll be fine," he said, and willed it straight to the mind of the Goddess so that She could make it true.

The corridor ended in a large arch, with wooden doors grown dark with age and agleam with generations of polish. Jeasa pushed on one of them and stepped back to allow him to enter. It was as he had come to expect: a long chamber with a vaulted roof held up with columns capped in lacy arches. The walls seemed entirely composed of windows . . . dark ones, the candlelight flickering off their lead bars. He wondered what the design and colors would be like in the morning. He hoped he would be in a position to appreciate them.

"Here, then," Jeasa said, stopping before the altar rail. There were no pews in the chapel, only a collection of triangular pillows stacked in the back. Like everything else in the house, it was too quiet. What would it be like for this household to be filled with people, instead of reflecting its dwindling populace with its oppressive silences?

"So," Vasiht'h said, drawing in a deep breath. "I'll take this . . . cup. And drink the stuff. And then while I'm in a semi-conscious state, five people will be studying and directing my thoughts. And then, in the morning, they'll decide whether I'm worthy, and this will be over."

"Yes," Jeasa said, solemn.

"All right," Vasiht'h said. "I guess it's not all that different from what Jahir and I do to our clients, in the end." He smiled crookedly. "There's some symmetry there. Or justice, maybe."

"You are a brave person," Jeasa said. "And I thank you for what you are doing for us."

Footsteps at the door distracted them both. Jahir was standing there with a cup: not just a cup, but a goblet made of some kind of silver metal, with amber and pearls inset on the walls.

Vasiht'h had no idea why he wanted to laugh: because the

cup was so absurd, so over-the-top, so ridiculous . . . or because it fit in with everything else around it, and he was the one who didn't belong in the fairy tale, and what did that suggest about him surviving?

But Jeasa was right: Jahir was upset.

/Arii,/ he sent, /I'll be fine./

Jahir entered with the cup and set it down in front of him. "I have to turn the mindline . . . well . . . off," he said. "They do not wish me to influence you."

"How 'off' is 'off'?" Vasiht'h asked uncertainly. Even at its lowest ebb, even with both of them blocking it, the mindline was still *there.* Losing that surety in his life would be upsetting.

"They shall have a priest at my side, holding me in abeyance," Jahir said. "So . . . functionally gone."

Vasiht'h swallowed. "All right. As long as it comes back."

"It will," Jahir promised, but Vasiht'h was painfully aware than neither of them was using the more intimate speech the mindline allowed . . . for fear, no doubt, of revealing their worries to one another.

"So," Vasiht'h said. "The cup."

Jahir handed it to him, as careful of his gloved fingers as if they had not spent years twining them in order to broaden the mindline and slip into the minds of their dreaming patients. Vasiht'h wondered if he was doing that to play to the audience no doubt hovering out of sight just beyond the chapel doors . . . or if it was another bid at keeping his fears to himself. The Glaseah made no remark, just took the cup and looked in it at the dark, glittering fluid. It smelled like grass. He wrinkled his nose and downed it all at once, swallowing around its acrid tingle. His throat wanted to contract around it.

Wiping his mouth, he handed the cup back with as much ceremony as he could muster and then settled down, paws tucked beneath his body and wings tightly folded to his back. He laced his fingers and let them hang against his lower chest.

"Good luck," Jeasa said softly, and withdrew.

Jahir hesitated.

"See you in the morning," Vasiht'h said firmly around the tingle-taste in his mouth.

Jahir drew in a breath . . . then smiled. "In the morning." And left, taking the cup with him and closing the door with a heavy and very final sound. A few moments later, the mindline vanished from his awareness, leaving him completely alone in his head for the first time in years.

That was far more distressing somehow than the fact that his body was trying to curl into a ball around his stomach. What had been in that cup? Maybe Jahir had been right: maybe it worked because it was poison. Maybe there had never been an out-worlder visitor to whatever-the-mouthful-of-a-name house . . . maybe they'd killed her for having the temerity to come here and be an alien at the Eldritch.

So why was he here?

Why had he even chosen Jahir?

Vasiht'h thought back to the day they'd met, at the border between the college campus and the children's hospital. He'd been tangled up in a jump-rope, letting a handful of children distract themselves from their sorrows by attempting to teach a clumsy "manylegs" to play their game . . . and out of nowhere, there had been a voice, assured, friendly, amused, asking if he could help. And he had . . . unthreading the rope Vasiht'h had been holding (surreptitiously) in his wing's thumb-joint and then joining him at the games, amusing the children until a pair of nurses had arrived to spirit away their delinquent charges.

Like everyone else in the Alliance, Vasiht'h had heard the rumors about Eldritch. He'd never expected to meet one. And when he had, Jahir had been nothing like those rumors. Not a single one of those stories had said anything about a sense of humor—often directed at himself when confronted with the Alliance's many challenges—nor had they said anything about that willingness to understand, to learn. The open heart that somehow lived comfortably with the Eldritch Veil. Perhaps, Vasiht'h thought, because Jahir was always helping someone, or listening to someone, and he knew very well that listening and helping were good ways to keep secrets.

Still, the magnitude of the secret Jahir had been keeping . . . Vasiht'h got to his legs, which were trembling in a way he found disconcerting, and tried pacing the length of the chapel. He felt strange, but not sick and not in immediate danger; surely that was a good sign.

So, the secret: the Eldritch were dying. They were *choosing* to die, by turning their backs on civilization, technology, new ideas, change of any kind. And amid this march to self-destruction, a small handful of individuals were fighting to prevent it; a fight, Vasiht'h thought, that Jahir would be obliged to take up himself, no matter his love of the Alliance and his idyll there. Seeing Jahir among his family, how seriously he took the duties of the heir, how easily he slipped into the role . . . the Glaseah knew it was only a matter of time. It might not be in Vasiht'h's lifetime—

—but then, it might. And the odds of that increased if he survived this ritual, because then he could be a part of it. A part of a struggle to revitalize an entire world. What would that be like?

Vasiht'h had never had any ambitions beyond going off his own world and finding something to do, something helpful. He was bewildered at the thought of having stumbled into an epic adventure, one suited entirely to the fairy tale halls of this Eldritch mansion.

His feet abruptly stopped working.

First one went numb. Then the other. A moment later he found himself pitching to the floor, spreading his wings to— what? Brake his fall? Ridiculous!

Flat on the ground, feeling his limbs oscillate between numbness and pins-and-needles, Vasiht'h wondered if he'd underestimated the toxicity of his drug. He licked his lips and found them dry, and his mouth as well. He tried to flex his fingers and found them only partially responsive. *Maybe,* he thought, *if they hurry, they can find me worthy of posthumous entrance into the family and then the wedding can go on anyway. Of course, they'd have to clear the corpse out of the chapel first . . .*

This brought on the inevitable question about what it would feel like, when the Eldritch in charge of making that determination slipped into his mind. The clients he and Jahir saw in their dream-therapy sessions reported not noticing, or seeing them represented in the dream itself, not as alien impressions, forced on them from outside . . . but as abstractions their own minds had created to explain the foreign presence. Would that be how it worked? Or would there be something more obvious? Something more high-handed?

Five people, he thought. One of them a priest of the God, one of them a representative of the Goddess, a priestess supposedly though he'd been confused at the explanation; the Goddess had a different kind of clergy than the God, or somesuch. And three people from the family. Jeasa maybe? He could hope for such gentleness. But maybe strangers. Vasiht'h tried to wrinkle his nose and thought he succeeded. The floor beneath him was very cold and very hard, and he'd fallen on his cheek with some of the fur against the grain, and it bothered him.

He was pondering whether to vomit when the chapel door opened. Confused, he looked toward the candles—they were still fresh, and the windows were still dark. It wasn't yet morning, so . . .

Sediryl swept in, wearing a black cloak over her gown. She knelt alongside him and began doing something that he didn't feel very accurately, but it involved laboring over his torso.

"Se . . . Sediryl?" he said weakly. "What are you doing here? No one is supposed to interrupt the vigil."

"I know," she said, grinning that feral grin at him. Her eyes were full of shadows; he couldn't read them. She resumed her work.

"You're . . . you're going to . . . ruin it—"

"I know," she said. "That's the point." She reached over and pried his jaws open, then shoved something—somethings?—so far down his throat he swallowed just to keep from gagging. "There, that should help."

"What . . ."

"An anti-toxin, among other things," she said, and waved away his protest. "I know, I shouldn't know there is one. I shouldn't know a lot of things, ah? But I do." She leaned closer, still grinning, but there wasn't the faintest shred of humor in her eyes. "I know all about this rite, since it was denied to me when I tried to make my lover part of the family, so I could properly marry him."

"What!" he hissed.

"Oh yes," Sediryl said. "You may be a terrible, awful out-worlder, friend Vasiht'h, but at least you're not human. If you want to find any alien more offensive to the Eldritch, you need look no further than Terra . . . where we were born."

"*What!*" he exclaimed again, so shocked he lost a few heart-beats. And then because the information was simply unbeliev-able, the word came out again, for emphasis. "What!"

"Oh yes," she said, laughing. "Just like your Pelted, we had human origins. Even worse: long, long ago we *were* human. But unlike the Pelted, we chose to divorce ourselves, and engineered our apartness to guarantee we could never go back. You Pelted had your existence forced on you by humans. We clawed ours free by force and fled our parent race. So, no, there would never be any returning for a human, and never any hope of one becoming family, no matter how much one of us might wish it. Even if we are closer kin to humans than we will ever be to a Harat-Shar pardine . . . or, Goddess! A creature like you." She slapped his back with something. "All right, up with you."

"I can't . . ." He stopped; he could feel his paws. "What did you give me?"

"I told you," she said. "An anti-toxin. You should be able to walk . . . carefully. I've hobbled you so don't take long steps."

"Why . . . why are you doing this?" Vasiht'h asked. "Sediryl!"

"You haven't asked what I'm doing yet," she said with a grin . . . and then hauled on the rope. To his dismay, the joints in his wings and arms sent spears of pain straight up his spine; he stumbled to his feet in sheer surprise and the pain subsided.

"What did you do to me!" he said.

"I tied you so I could control you, of course," she said. "I figured you wouldn't come if I asked." She bounced the rope lightly on his back. "Do what I tell you to and I won't pull."

"You haven't left me much of a choice," he said from between gritted teeth.

"Yes, well. . . . no," she said, and laughed. "Now walk."

"Where are we going?" he asked, but he obeyed, fighting anger and distress. Sensation had returned to his limbs; he could feel where she'd knotted his hands behind his humanoid back, wrapping the rope around his waist as well as his wrists. Then there was some kind of complex arrangement trapping his wings against his spine . . . it hurt just trying to tug them free.

"Don't bother," she said. "You'll just make the knots tighter."

"So you learned bondage in the Alliance, is that it?" he hissed.

"I'm surprised you even know about bondage, given the Glaseahn disinterest in sex," she said with insane cheer. "Now get on, there, pony."

"You left my mouth free," Vasiht'h said. "What's to keep me from screaming?"

"You can scream all you want," she said. "No one will hear. They're all off in a padded room, listening for your thoughts and wondering why they can't hear them." She laughed. "I've been hoping for an opportunity like this for so long . . . they have no idea how well I've planned it."

"Planned what?" Vasiht'h finally asked.

"Their comeuppance," she said, and slapped his back with the rope. "Now move."

As he walked, Vasiht'h grasped frantically for the mindline and found it dead. Not all the hauling, the stamping, the wishing or the reaching forced it open . . . and he had no idea how to mindspeak the other Eldritch, though he tried, calling for them as loudly as he could.

"No doubt," Sediryl said as she guided him through the halls for all the worlds like a carriage-driver directing her horses, "you are trying very hard to tell Jahir or anyone else what's befallen you." She pursed her lips, looking up at the ceiling, and piped, "

'Help! The madwoman has abducted me!' " She laughed. "Don't bother. The anti-toxin wasn't the only pill I slipped you. The other will cancel your mental abilities. No use doing all this if they can hear you in other ways and come to your rescue, ah?"

"You thought of everything," Vasiht'h said, his mood foul.

"That I have," she said cheerily, and slapped his rump with the rope. "Get along now." She paused, then added, "I believe I'm even having fun."

"I'm glad one of us is," Vasiht'h muttered.

Fight her! something whispered. He shook his head, trying to clear the thought from it. There was no use fighting. Not only would it not accomplish anything, except maybe to tie the knots tighter and hurt him worse, but he was no fighter. He was a healer, and while half his arsenal had been neutralized by her esper-blanking pill (and who had ever heard of such a thing! Why had it never made the news, particularly among his esper people?), the other half . . . the more important half . . . she'd left him.

He could still talk.

"So a comeuppance," he said as they marched out of the mansion into a clear, cool spring night. The stars were a revelation; it had been a while since he'd been on a planet with atmosphere. The twinkling was beautiful, like gemstones throwing off sparkles. "Revenge for a spurned lover?"

"Don't be ridiculous," Sediryl said. "I'm not avenging him. I'm avenging myself. On this entire debased culture. On a society that could call me a fallen woman for loving and daring to consummate that love. On a people who could mock me for making a mistake, to my face! And drive me from my own homeworld with their ridicule."

Something about that felt wrong. Didn't it? He'd barely met her, but he thought he'd taken her tenor, and this felt far too violent for his observations. Wasn't it? "You don't seem like the kind of person who could be driven anywhere."

She snorted. "You don't know me very well, then. Go on, into the trees."

"Where are we going?" Vasiht'h asked.

"Not your concern."

He wanted to point out that it was very much his concern, but doing so wouldn't get him anywhere. "Interrupting the rite doesn't seem a very useful way to punish the people who hurt you," he said instead. "If I fail, it's your family that'll suffer, while the people I'd think you would hate—the xenophobic, backwards ones—are the ones who'll benefit, because then they can break off the wedding and keep the alien influence at bay."

Why are you bothering with this? She's a lost cause.

Which was a thought he would never have had under normal circumstances . . . maybe he was going mad? Then again, he'd never been kidnapped before; Goddess knew what stresses he was under. He twitched his flanks as if to remove an offending fly, thinking that no one was a lost cause, who still lived. Sediryl was in pain. Maybe he could help.

"You think like a mortal," Sediryl said with a sigh. At the narrow-eyed glance he threw over his shoulder, she said, "That's what Eldritch call you short-lived species, you know. *Gathanaes*, "mortal." As if we were somehow less mortal just for living ten times as long." Her smile was thin. "Nevertheless. You're thinking too small, Vasiht'h. My aim is not the destruction of this wedding. It's the destruction of this race."

He remembered, sudden and ice-shocking, her off-hand comment about a civil war culling the species. Maybe he'd been wrong about her? But he'd been so sure.

"You see," she continued airily, "if I disrupt the wedding, it won't go through. The xenophobes will win. And if I disrupt it the right way . . . well. I'll ensure that no outworlder will ever come here again. And then the society will collapse, Vasiht'h, and the Eldritch will die . . . and I will finally have my revenge."

"You would kill an entire species in a fit of pique?" Vasiht'h said, horrified.

The abrupt yank on his rope made him fall to one knee from the pain. Sediryl lunged in front of him and hissed, "It's not *pique*. It's *justice*. It's removing a mistake from the universe. And I won't be the only one doing it . . . the entire species will abet me. The blame won't be mine alone." She pulled back, eyes burning. "Do you understand now? I might set this all in motion, but if they choose to stop it . . . if they grow enough to deserve to live . . . then they can still do it. But if they remain benighted and sick, then they will career down the road I am about to lay down for them, and they will have deserved that too. It's perfect." She lifted her chin, voice gone cold. "I'm no simple storybook villain, Vasiht'h. I'm the pivot that history will turn on. Either I will become the midwife to our rebirth . . . or I will be the blacksmith who makes the sword we turn on our own necks."

"Sediryl," Vasiht'h said desperately, "you can't do this."

"Give me one good reason why not," she said.

"Because," he said, "it's wrong. It's wrong, to take away other people's choices. It's wrong to play at being a goddess. We're not meant for such powers."

She smiled. "You aren't, maybe, with your so-short lifespan. But me?" She straightened and tugged him toward a tree. He limped after her, desperate and feeling as if one of his wing-arms was only precariously still in its socket after her last punishment.

"You never did ask," she said as she tied him fast to the trunk, "how I was going to precipitate my grand plan. How I was going to ensure that no offworlder would ever choose to come back."

His heart was pounding painfully. "You really don't have to tell me."

"Ah, but then you wouldn't know!" she said, smiling. She leaned forward. "A gruesome murder. Something horrific enough to make the Alliance label this world off-limits. Maybe even something bad enough to damage the treaty? We'll see."

Vasiht'h met her eyes. "You are not a murderer."

She paused at that. Then lifted her brows. "You're so certain."

"Yes," Vasiht'h said. "I am."

"Even though I'm planning the murder of my entire race?" Sediryl said casually, swinging the remains of the rope so it smacked his side. It distracted him, the little pinch of pain at his wing joints, the constant blows, but he focused on what he felt, knew, believed with all his heart was the truth. She had not been able to think of herself as her race's murderer, or she would not have concocted the entire fiction about being its midwife, about the possibility of its transformation. And even in that myth, her dark side had not been the murderer, but the manufacturer of the weapon the race would use to suicide.

"You are not a murderer," he repeated, certain as Aksivaht'h had breath.

She met his eyes, held them.

Then she grinned. "You're right, I'm not."

He blew out a breath in relief.

"But I'm also not above letting other people . . . or in this case, other animals . . . do my dirty work," she said, and his guts knotted. She checked her work, tugging here and there to make sure he was well and truly affixed to his tree. "There are animals in these woods that will rip you apart in a fashion most spectacular. Far better than I could, anyway, with my poor imagination for such things. All I have to do . . ." She drew a knife from the shadows of her cloak. ". . . is invite them." A flash of starlight against keen edge and pain sprang up all along his side. "I believe if they aim here they'll get your organs, yes? You'll probably die slowly, unless they find that thing you use for a secondary heart down between your forelegs."

"If they find me ripped apart by animals, they won't blame the Eldritch," Vasiht'h said, gasping. "Your plan will fail."

Sediryl chuckled. "You just keep trying, don't you." She tossed the knife on the ground. "There are Eldritch footprints here. There's a knife conveniently stamped with a centicore and enameled in green and electrum. You are tied to the tree with knots that, I assure you, were not tied by animal paws. If some horde of predators devoured your carcass after you were murdered by an Eldritch who dragged you to the middle of nowhere to kill you, well . . . you are in the middle of the woods at night." She studied him and nodded, eyes lighting with satisfaction. "You probably have a half hour or so before they pick up your scent, maybe less. You have enough time to pray to your goddess to accept you back into her mind, if you're so inclined."

He said nothing, staring at her while the blood drained, hot and swift, down the curve of his belly.

"What, no last words? No comments?" she said. "I at least expected an 'I hate you!'"

"I don't hate you, Sediryl," Vasiht'h said, quiet. "I feel sorry for you. I'm sorry that you hurt so badly. I'm sorry that you've been driven to this place. And above all, I'm sorry that no one was there for you, to help you work through your hurt before it could poison you this way."

"Pity," Sediryl said. "How tiresome, and how predictable." She smiled. "Farewell, friend Vasiht'h."

This was not how he had planned to die.

No, this was not how he had planned to die. Goddess knew, he hadn't even believed the poison would kill him . . . not truly, not in his heart. He'd expected to spend the rest of his life with Jahir. Maybe find a priestess to give him children to take them back to the starbase to raise. But not to chain Jahir, the way the Royal Tams seemed to have chained their Eldritch, with generations of children as . . . as some kind of hairshirt. No, he thought with a fond, but faint, smile, it was far more likely that his children would have become Jahir's rather than the other way around . . . a generational army of Glaseah to help him settle this world's problems properly. Surely that's all the world needed . . . a good, long, multiple-mortal-lifetime therapy session.

How can you laugh when you're bleeding to death?

And that was a question he didn't know how to answer. Maybe it was the mental image of Jahir with Glaseahn kits sleeping on his stomach. Or the image of Jahir accompanied by a long line of Glaseah, growing up as they marched alongside him, growing old, dying, and being replaced by fresh versions. A renewable resource, like seeds from a favored tree.

Doesn't that idea bother you? You hated the thought of Lesandurel being chained to the Tam-illee family. But you would indenture your own scions to an Eldritch?

It wasn't indenture. It was service. Willing service, it would have to be . . . but then, he'd probably have enough children that at least one would be willing. Really, who wouldn't? The opportunity of a lifetime, something out of a book . . . to save a world.

Assuming all your children are therapists . . .

Not even that, he thought. There would be work for engineers, and linguists, for chefs and maids, for agronomists, for scientists, for administrators . . . and just for people, to be friends, to be Jahir's sanity. The way he was.

Or at least, the way he had been supposed to be, before Sediryl dragged him out here. And now, if he died, all of that future would be forfeit. And Jahir would be left alone. That was surely the worst.

The worst? So is Jahir more important to you than his world?

That question gave him pause. He looked up at what stars he could see through the thin new leaves, some of them so young he could see the star-glow through them, just. "There's no separating them," he said. "I know that now. I can have Jahir, and his world alive and thriving . . . or I have neither." He sighed out, looking down at the knots tying him to the tree and trying to flex his wrists. "I made my choice. To be honest, I made it years ago, that first day that I met him, that I saw him trying to make some terminally sick children laugh. I already love him, and . . . loving someone means you inherit their family." He closed his eyes, trying to lean back against the trunk, to ease the pressure on his spine. "I would have gladly done it. Made formal what already is. But even if I can't . . . nothing will take away that it already is. Recognized by rite or not."

The blood seeped down the curve of his side, dripped onto the duff. Eventually, it drew the feeling from his extremities with it, and it grew harder to think. *Not much time,* he thought, and opened his eyes . . . on the knife.

Which was close enough to his paw to reach. Could he? No, there was no way to get it to his hands, and he couldn't use it with a paw.

. . . but maybe, just maybe . . . he could bury it. The knots would still remain to attest to an Eldritch's hand, but if the knife was missing, they wouldn't conclude past any doubt that the groom's family had to have done it . . . would they?

It was worth a chance. To give the world some slim hope of surviving him, it was worth it.

Marshaling the last of his strength, Vasiht'h began to paw a hole in the dirt. He was still digging when his consciousness began to fail.

No! *he thought.* Not before I finish! Please, Goddess! Let me at least do this one thing . . . please—

———∞———

"Arii! ARII! Stop fighting me, it's well, it's *all right*—" /Vasiht'h! You're safe!/

Vasiht'h stopped struggling against the arms, and doing so made it clear they were not holding him down, but embracing him. An embrace he found familiar, though he'd only felt it on the rarest of occasions. He and Jahir touched hands frequently in their work, but to hold one another was something reserved for the most acute of emotions.

The relief he felt at being alive, at being reunited with his friend, was definitely, definitely acute. He pressed his head into Jahir's much broader shoulder and dug his fingers into the Eldritch's back. "You're here! I'm here! I . . . wait . . . what . . . the ritual!"

"You passed," another voice said, and he stiffened in panic as Sediryl grinned at him from behind Jahir's back.

At the panic that threatened to shatter the mindline, Jahir said, "No, no! It's all right! Everything that happened was part of the rite."

"W-what?"

"We had to test you," Sediryl said. "And everyone agreed that I would make the most credible villain for the piece, a far better one than, say, one of the groom's family. Jahir said you wouldn't fall quite so hard for the obvious hatred, and would have an easier time believing something more . . . um . . . psychiatric."

"Then you . . ."

". . . didn't tie you up and leave you for the wild animals," Sediryl said, laughing. "That was just the scenario we played out. Even then, I think you almost guessed it wasn't real a couple of times."

Vasiht'h leaned back, hands on Jahir's arms. He looked away from his beloved partner's face . . . saw sunlight streaming through the stained glass. As he expected, it was beautiful. "Then . . . I passed?"

"You passed," Jahir agreed, voice rough with something that the mindline rendered as dawn breaking, as a relief heady as the cradling arms of a mother.

"I passed," Vasiht'h whispered, and tried not to wobble. "I think I'm going to throw up . . ."

Jahir laughed and gathered his upper body close again, and Vasiht'h rested his nose against that warm alien hair and breathed in the strange-familiar incense smell of it and ignored the bump of a no-doubt priceless blue pearl against his muzzle and just smiled. Smiled, and relaxed, and maybe squeezed a little water from under his lashes.

And when he could, he whispered, unrepentant and a great deal triumphant, /Told you I'd be fine./

/You were right,/ Jahir said, his laugh rueful but bright, like yellow flowers nodding in the spring sunshine. /I'll listen next time./

/I'll hold you to that!/

"The family is satisfied," Jeasa said from the door. "There remains only the formality."

Vasiht'h straightened, releasing Jahir and hoping no one else had seen their no doubt utterly inappropriate embrace. "Ma'am?"

"Vasiht'h, as head of the Seni Galare, I am pleased to extend to you the invitation of kinship. Do you still desire it?"

"I do!" Vasiht'h said, the words filling the mindline, spreading out, spilling like sunshine. "I do."

She came forth then with a medallion strung on a long silver chain, which she looped around his neck. "Then be welcome to the family. We will write your name in the book, and no one shall challenge your right to walk among us again."

The medallion dropped onto his chest, cool against his fur. He picked it up and twisted it to look: a cloisonné unicorn on bright blue enamel background. At least, he thought gratefully, it wasn't made of some unspeakably precious stone; that would have made wearing it on the starbase somewhat more conspicuous than he liked.

/It's a lot less conspicuous than it could be,/ Jahir said.

/They come more obvious than this?/ Vasiht'h said, bemused.

/Oh yes,/ Jahir answered, amused. /Remind me to tell you a little history one day about the link between the Galare house medallions and the far more ostentatious amulets rampant./ At the feel of Vasiht'h's disbelief, he added, /You can always take it off when we get home./

/After how hard I worked for this?/ Vasiht'h said. /I don't think so . . . !/

Jahir grinned.

"And now, if you feel able, kinsman," Jeasa said. "We should present you to the rest of the family . . ."

". . . starting, I hope, with me," said a new voice in flawless Universal.

At his side, Jahir twisted and went instantly to one knee, hand on the thigh and head bent with hair shrouding his face. Jeasa dropped into a deep curtsey and did not rise, and Sediryl gained her feet to do the same. Slowly, he looked up at the owner of that voice, and even without the crown and scepter he would have recognized her. In truth, the trappings were superfluous. The steel in the woman's mien and the aura of power that radiated like heat from the furnace of a sun were all the scepter and crown she needed. With them alone she could rule the world— did rule it.

"Ah . . . Your . . . Majesty?" Vasiht'h managed, grateful that he was already sort of kneeling already.

"And you, the first outworlder to use Sellelvi's rite since it was created for her," the Queen of the Eldritch said, "you are . . . ?"

"Vasiht'h," he answered, meek, and then with a touch of

stubborn pride, "Vasiht'h Seni Galare."

Liolesa laughed, and a sound of such richness he'd rarely heard: satisfaction, self-assurance, amusement, power . . . a matching pride. Goddess! he thought. No wonder Jeasa spoke of civil wars. Such a woman would inspire deathless allegiance, or utter defiance, for she would steamroll anyone of lesser conviction.

"Yes, indeed," she said. "And as the head of the Galare House, I welcome you to it. You've chosen well . . ." Her eyes drifted to Jahir's bent head. "And this, your choice, yes?"

"Yes," Vasiht'h said, fierce.

"And you, then, heir to the Seni?"

"Your Majesty," Jahir said and hesitated. Then said, finally, "I am content."

"You've done well in your wanders," Liolesa said. "And better yet, to bring your treasures home. We trust you will do so one day for good."

Vasiht'h's mouth went dry at the implied command. He'd figured out what he thought Jahir was about, but he hadn't expected it to be brought into the open quite so soon.

Unperturbed, Jahir replied, "My Queen, when the time is right."

So much through the mindline, but mostly the clarion sound of the address: not of a man to his queen, but of a vassal to his liegelady. So few words, to be so clear a promise, and with it, the ordering of both their fates for all their lives before them.

/Do you regret it?/ Jahir whispered.

/No,/ Vasiht'h said, and put all his truth behind the word.

/My dear,/ Jahir said. /I still think this is more than you bargained for./

/What else?/ Vasiht'h answered. /The Goddess needs some room to work./

Jahir laughed silently.

Liolesa had turned to Jeasa. "Seni Galare, rise." When the woman had done so, she said, "I had heard there was a wedding . . . ?"

"There may have been such a rumor, my Queen," Jeasa answered with a flicker of a smile.

"A wedding requires a representative of the Lady, does it not?" Liolesa said. "Why, do you suppose there would be any trouble with my offering my services?"

Jeasa laughed. "My lady, I think no one would stop you even if they did."

"Just so," Liolesa said with a fire in her eyes that was rather more ferocious than Vasiht'h would have liked directed at him. "Please do me the honor of introducing me to the guests."

"My Queen," Jeasa said with relish, "the honor would be mine."

The wedding was, in retrospect, anti-climactic. Vasiht'h was still a little wobbly from the drug's aftereffects ("Sorry," Sediryl had said, "the anti-toxin bit was a fiction."), but he'd recovered enough to brush out his fur, don the orange sari with its gilt, patterned edges, and arrange the new House medallion over the top. He'd even secured a couple of sleigh bells from Jeasa and hung them on his wing thumb-joints, though he was feeling ambivalent about wishing fertility on two pre-pubescent children . . . one of whom couldn't even be convinced to stand near his bride, because she was a *girl*.

During the reception that followed, Vasiht'h stayed near Jahir and watched the Queen work the room. She was too far from him for Jahir's mind to catch any of the conversations, but even the restrained Eldritch were subject to the laws of humanoid body language, and Vasiht'h had had years of practice reading Jahir. Everywhere Liolesa went, he saw people bend to her; whether they started out ruffled and resentful and outraged, or whether they were already hers before she spoke, they all showed signs of respect or submission by the end of the conversation . . . and all without the Queen making any noises other than those indicating courtesy and modest emotion. She owned the room, as she had the house the moment she entered it. Had the groom's family entertained any notion of reneging on the wedding because the bride's family had had the poor taste to make an outworlder kin, Liolesa's arrival had blown all such plans out of the water. One did not manufacture flimsy excuses against a union when one's sovereign arrived to play its priestess for their son.

It made him wonder how she'd known to come, and how she'd gotten here so quickly . . . and with guards to boot; his gaze wandered toward the doors where the stern-faced men with swords were standing, unobtrusive but somehow very, very obvious. But however she'd done it, he found himself selfishly glad; with the Queen of the world in the room, no one was paying any attention to *him*.

⸙⸙⸙

As the night advanced the reception began to diffuse into the household, and from there onto the grounds. Some of the guests retired, and some took their discussions elsewhere. Vasiht'h heard the echoes of music in the halls, finally filling them with something more lively than the lonely footsteps he'd come to expect. Seeing Jahir occupied with a few peers, Vasiht'h slipped out of the hall. He was halfway down it when he thought better of sneaking out completely unnoticed and whispered, /*I'm going to get some fresh air.*/

/*You sure you're entirely steady on your feet?*/

He smiled as he passed through the foyer. /*I'll be fine.*/ And feeling the steel-brushed finish of his partner's wry humor, added, /*What?*/

/*Just wondering how you can find the outside so comforting so soon after the rite.*/

/*Oh!*/ Vasiht'h walked through the great doors and looked up at the vault of the sky. In lieu of answering, he let the mindline absorb his wonder at the sight of that glittering vista: so many stars, winking at him, as if sharing their ancient secrets. The hard vacuum starfield visible outside most of the starbase's great windows seemed without character in compare.

/*Ah,*/ Jahir answered with a smile he could feel like the gleam of a full moon. */I'll see you presently, then, my dear./*

Vasiht'h nodded, pleased, and let his feet wander. He avoided people's voices, and took it slowly, getting used to his own skin again, to being whole, to being alive and out of danger . . . to being . . . well, kin to an Eldritch, and now allowed the liberty of the house without anyone's objection. He glanced over his shoulder at the manor, at the lamps burning in the windows, the glitter cut by the sharp edges of beveled glass. Such a beautiful place to be so empty, and so old, so long to yearn for renewal and change. So much to be addressed. He sighed . . . and chuckled a little also, and turned back to the long path leading toward the commons.

There, once again, he found a distant figure, dwindling and familiar. He squinted at it, frowned, then hurried after it.

"Sediryl!" he called, and she reined in the horse. No pony this, but a tall, fine-limbed creature whose shoulder was well over Vasiht'h's. He slowed a few respectful body-lengths away from it and approached more cautiously. When she glanced at him and reined the horse in, he looked up into her face and searched her eyes . . . and was gratified by what he saw there. His instincts had been right; no matter how bitter she was, her frustrations with this world were rooted in her love for it. No murderer, Sediryl. He wondered when she'd be back to help Jahir change it. "Sediryl? Where are you going? It's late for a ride."

"I'm not on a pleasure jaunt, Vasiht'h," she said. "Or should I say 'cousin' now, maybe?"

"I'd like that," he admitted. "It's appropriate."

"Cousin, then," Sediryl said. The hood of her cloak was pooled at the back of her shoulders, reminding him strongly of her appearance in the ritual. "I'm on my way home."

"You're leaving already?" Vasiht'h said. "But . . . the reception's not even over . . ."

"It's close enough," Sediryl said, "and I have no reason to stay. I already said my farewells, my aunt knows I've left."

"Jahir didn't tell me you were leaving . . . ," Vasiht'h said, confused. "I would have come to say goodbye—"

"Why would I tell Jahir?" Sediryl asked, head canted.

And then he realized, a horrible, slow thick realization, that she didn't know. Hadn't known how Jahir felt about her . . . until now. He saw it break over her face, animate her too-fierce eyes as she looked down at him in surprise.

"Oh, Goddess!" Vasiht'h exclaimed, holding out his hands so suddenly the horse shied. "Please, don't say a word! Don't tell him I told you!"

"You didn't tell me," Sediryl said, but her words were slow, and her gaze was entirely internalized . . . on what great shift inside herself, Vasiht'h hardly dared guess. "I figured it out." She grinned, and as abruptly as that she was in the moment again, wearing her glib mask. "That's the problem with family. It's so hard to keep secrets from them."

"Sediryl . . ."

She shook her head, gathering the reins in her slim gloved hands. "No, Vasiht'h—cousin. Don't ask."

Of course, that made him desperately want to. But the more he looked at her face, the more he read the grim determination in her voice and the tension of her hands, the more he understood that he didn't have to. Instead, he said, "He'll regret not having seen you off."

"No, he won't," Sediryl said. "Cousin, what I said to you outside the commons is still true. Jahir is a true son of this world, and will be back. But there won't be any coming back for me. I'm not wanted, and I don't belong." Her smile grew crooked and sad, and he thought of a tree grown into a strange shape, seeking light it couldn't find. "My desires have never been honored by my homeworld. My choice is to stay here, and be denied until I grow sick with unfulfilled needs . . . or to find my own way. I've made my choice." She shook her head and finished, quieter, "No matter what I want, my path doesn't lead back here."

To that, he could find nothing to say . . . nothing she would believe. So he let her press her heels against the horse's barrel, the stirrup leather squeaking, and watched as the dark shrouded her, shadows stealing up her black cloak as she drew away.

"I'll tell him you said goodbye," he called.

She laughed, and didn't look back.

∽∽∽

Vasiht'h was in the nest of pillows that night long before Jahir returned. He had time to tour his partner's suite, to scrutinize the furniture, the tapestries, the instruments, the books . . . to examine and see that Sediryl had been right about them. He'd gone to his bed thoughtful, and grateful to have something soft to lie on after the chapel's unforgiving floor.

He woke when Jahir quietly closed the suite's door behind him. Struggling to one elbow, he peered past the pillows to see his friend sit on the divan in the common room to begin stripping off his boots.

/*Things go all right?*/ he asked, not wanting to break the starlit silence.

/*As well as could be expected, given the excitement,*/ Jahir answered, his voice faded with distraction. /*Tomorrow the groom's family will depart, and take Juzie with them. The Queen will leave also. And you and I . . . we should think about leaving ourselves.*/ He sighed and straightened. /*I don't know about you, but I'm ready to be gone. I miss Veta.*/

/*Me too,*/ Vasiht'h said, and withdrew from the conversation to let his partner bathe and prepare for bed in silence. He didn't speak again until Jahir's silhouette darkened the entry to the bedroom. "I'm glad we came."

Jahir paused in the act of tucking his robe more closely around. "You are?"

Vasiht'h nodded. "I miss Veta too, and I'll be glad to be gone. But yes. I'm glad we came. And Jahir . . . I'll keep your secrets. Even the one about humanity." He lifted his head to meet the Eldritch's eyes. "That one was true, wasn't it."

Jahir hesitated. Then smiled faintly and sat on the step-stool leading up to the mattress. "Yes."

Vasiht'h nodded. "She had to throw some truth in there to keep it believable, I guess."

"Just so," Jahir said. And after a moment, said, "Thank you. For the promise."

"Our secrets now," Vasiht'h said. "Not yours. That should make things easier."

"Yes."

Vasiht'h offered him his hand. Jahir reached across the gulf and took it, winding his long white fingers in Vasiht'h's shorter furred ones. They shared the heartbeat subjectivity of time through their touch, and more sublime things as well. If there was grief for the inevitable heartbreak in their future . . . well. There was wisdom in all the Goddess's creations, sorrow no less than joy.

"So about that girl with the spotted back," Jahir began.

"Oh no," Vasiht'h said. "I haven't even settled into the family I've just gotten, I am not starting a new one!"

Jahir laughed and climbed into the bed. "Goodnight, Vasiht'h Seni Galare."

"Goodnight, arii," Vasiht'h said.

/I still think she was adorable./

Vasiht'h kicked the mindline, and ignored the soft chuckle from the bed as he curled up on the pillows to sleep.

Author's Note

*This short story takes place roughly a year
after the events of the novel* Dreamstorm *and
several before the events of "Family."*

HEALING WATERS

/And, alet. When you are no longer raw. When you have a center to move from. You come to me, and I will share what it is like. To taste/ hear through the water./

OME DOWN," THE REPLY SAID, and so Jahir found himself standing before the entrance to Mercy Hospital's rehabilitation wing, basking in the heat of Heliocentrus's summer and marshaling his every breath against the gravity. He'd thought memory would prepare him for its punishing weight, but memory, he discovered, could dim. But he bore it better than he had then, for he came now as a man no longer divided against his own heart. Vasiht'h had not elected to make this trip with him, but their years together on Veta had made whole in Jahir much of what had been fragile and tender; he found the sight of Mercy affecting, but not harrowing; more than that, he was glad to be back, even if only for a few days, to keep a promise long in the fulfillment. He'd intended to return far sooner, but the years had slipped past, and then after he'd renewed his resolve following the disaster at Tsera Nova, still it had needed nearly a year before he felt able to pry himself from the routine that structured his life.

But at last he'd sent the question, and been accepted, and here he was. Passing through the doors, Jahir headed for the pool.

The facilities were just as he recalled them, without even the wear that the passage of time should have wrought, but then . . . this was the Alliance, and this in particular its winter capital. Mercy would never fall into disrepair, not so long as there was a single Pelted to walk its city's thoroughfares. The pool stretched before him, a vast thing beneath a transparent roof, the light bright on the waters that shifted as its patients carried out their regimens beneath the vigilant eyes of their therapists. Private pools were available along one wall, the doors leading into them discreetly closed, and there was a passthrough to the hospital at the far end of the building, along with the rooms for dry therapy. Changing rooms, however, were at this end, along with the therapists' offices, and it was there Jahir went, guided by memory unblemished by time. He paused at Shellie Aralyn's door and said, "Alet, it is good to see you again."

The Asanii turned, and her eyes brightened. "Well, see what the space wind blew in! And Sun and Stars, look at you. Healthy as a weed."

Jahir chuckled. "Freshly come from the orbital station, else I fear I would be wilting. I remain unsuited to the gravity despite the ultimate success of the acclimatization."

Aralyn had left her desk to join him, studying him critically. "You really do look good. Living someplace a little lighter, I'm guessing?"

"Starbase Veta."

"Ah, yes, that would do it." She grinned. "Standard gravity is kinder. I'm guessing you're here for Paga?"

"I am, yes. He said I might just come by?"

"I'm sure he did." She chortled. "He's looking forward to this."

"I am glad to hear it. . . ."

"Every year or so, he mentions you," she continued. "'That Eldritch will come by. You'll see.'" She flashed him a lopsided smile. "Only because I tease him about it. The return of the impossible Eldritch."

"Not so impossible," Jahir promised. "See, here I am."

"So you are. Go ahead and get changed . . . he's almost done. You remember where it is."

"I do, yes," he said. And paused, because in the lapses between her animated responses there was a gulf that troubled him, and a faint smudge beneath her eyes hinted at poor nights. "I find you well, alet?"

"Of course," she said. "Just the usual ups and downs. It's a hard profession. You know."

"I do," he said, because even if he hadn't worked at Mercy he would now have had his experiences at Veta's General to inform his opinion. "I'll change."

Was it strange to return to the cubicle where he'd once marveled at the technology that would supply him with swim-wear from a scan of his body? He set his bag down and pulled out the suit he used as a matter of course, and the towel, and began the laborious process of divesting himself of the layers he wore against the cold in most Alliance's common spaces. He remembered powerfully standing here, his exhaustion and the poignancy of doing work he believed in, but at such cost. Of finding almost no surcease, save in the waters of this pool . . . and in Vasiht'h, once his friend had arrived, crossing the worlds to follow him. Jahir smiled. How fortunate he was, and how endlessly grateful.

Securing his bag in a locker, Jahir padded to the pool and sat on its edge, careful of his too-heavy limbs, to await his host. To sit here and allow the reflections off the water to fill his eyes and clear his mind . . . no hardship.

Paga did not keep him waiting long, though. The Naysha's head popped from the water in front of him, enormous green eyes gleaming. Bringing his hands up, the Naysha signed, /Here at last./

"I'm sorry for the wait," Jahir began, but Paga patted the water, interrupting him.

/All things for a reason. This is the right time to be here./ A wide grin, showing off a predator's teeth. */No need to understand the reasons. Yes?/*

"Yes," Jahir agreed.

/Stay./ The Naysha forged to the other side of the pool and half-lifted himself from it, a startling display: few people saw Naysha out of water, and their size always came as a surprise. They were not small people . . . the average male was some nine feet long, and all of it hard muscle, more like a dolphin than the slender fish-tailed merfolk of human legend.

The Naysha's imperious slap brought Aralyn's head from the door.

"Oh, you found him?"

/Yes. Send luggage ahead? I take him home my way./

"Oh, sure. Alet, will you release your bag to me? I'll make arrangements."

Startled, Jahir said, "I was planning on returning to the station for the evening?"

Paga snorted. */Absolutely not. You stay with me. Guest. Been so long, least I can do. Yes?/*

Useless to ask whether he could be accommodated, for surely the Naysha would not have offered otherwise. And yet either his pause or the situation was leading enough for Aralyn to smile a lopsided smile. "I've stayed there a few times. You'll like it."

"Then I am honored to accept."

A few moments was all that was necessary to fetch forth his bag and hand it to Aralyn . . . not without a pang, for even knowing the innocuousness of his clothes and the privacy locks common to data tablets, he still felt uncomfortable giving so much of himself away to an acquaintance. But then the Naysha was beckoning him to the water, and as always the adventure of life in the Alliance called him, and he answered.

/Into the water,/ the Naysha said. */Easier for you than walking./*

It was, and he welcomed the respite, no matter how slight, from Selnor's pitiless gravity. Paga watched as Jahir slid into the water, the Naysha's enormous eyes appraising. */Look good. Muscle tone very good, consistent with habitual swimmer. Much practice, I* *see./*

"It helps," Jahir said. "So I have taken care not to let my practice lapse." He thought of Vasiht'h, smiled. "When I am so careless of myself to do so, I am reminded."

The Naysha smacked the water, mouth gaping. */That Glaseah./*

Jahir smiled. "Yes. That Glaseah."

Paga nodded. */Come./* And turning, started for the end of the pool.

No matter how much easier it was to swim the length of the gym than to walk it, the exercise still struck Jahir as frivolous; to get wet when he could have stayed dry, and dressed, and carried his own bag? But that puzzlement lasted only to the end of the pool, when the Naysha paused, bobbing in the water, to sign, / *Hold breath only a moment. Air on other side. All right?/*

Mystified, Jahir said, "Yes."

Paga nodded and vanished under the surface, and Jahir followed as bade.

Against the wall of the pool was a round egress, complete with palm sensor. Paga pressed a hand to it, then ducked through with a powerful flap of his tail. Jahir waited for the air bubbles to clear and pulled himself after—

—and felt a whole-body tingle—

—and then he was breaking the surface of a small calm pool beneath a cupola of clear glass through which the dipping sun could be seen coloring Heliocentrus's glorious sea scarlet. He gasped in, startled. Paga had to splash him to draw his attention. */Staging area. All aquatics who work in the hospital pass through here, with the water-lock to Mercy's pool. This is . . ./* A sudden grin. */My commute./*

"How beautiful!" Jahir said, low.

/Also fun,/ Paga said. */You will see. Come./*

The chamber had six different exits, transparent tunnels partially filled with running water. On one side of each tunnel, the current ran toward the staging area, and on the other, away. This was the side Paga pulled himself onto, holding himself in place with a fin so he could look back and sign, */Not far. Enjoy the ride./*

With that, the Naysha let go and was carried away. Startled, Jahir pulled himself after, and found himself coasting in luke-warm water, comfortable as an embrace and more exhilarating by far. Above, the flexglass offered an uninterrupted view of the sky, the surrounding landscaping, and soon the beach, whisking past beneath his wondering gaze.

Paga snagged him by the wrist, arresting him before he could continue on, and pulled him down a side corridor. A few flicks of his tail, and they were passing through an ingress and into another circular chamber, this one with a round pool set under a loft. The pool was surrounded by a crete ledge, one broad enough for several bonsai, a computer interface, and what Jahir could only guess was a kitchen, with counters low enough to be accessed from the water. But the view . . . the view was most cer-tainly the attraction, for while the hemisphere behind the loft was solid, the opposite was open to one of Heliocentrus's white beaches, close enough to the surf for the foaming waves to plash, now and then, against the flexglass wall.

"Oh, alet!" Jahir breathed.

The Naysha came alongside him, holding himself upright. /
Beautiful, yes?/

"Unspeakably so. Do you . . . can you go to the sea?"

/*Access underwater./* Another grin. /*True waterlock there. Don't want sleeping waters and ocean waters mixing. Also, tide would make problems with water level in apartment. And small creatures visiting. Get trapped./*

Surprised, Jahir laughed. "God and Lady! I imagine that might be awkward."

/*Worst is octopus. Chasing octopus out is impossible. They are too curious./* Paga pointed to the loft, the blueish webbing between his forefinger and thumb stretched taut. /*Bed up there for dry-landers. You can stay there. Need anything particular?/*

Usually he wanted blankets, but the temperature in the Nay-sha's apartment was far warmer than Alliance norm, and humid. "No, I think this will be delightful. Do all the apartments have those lofts?"

/Many but not all. I particularly wanted it. For visitors./
"Aralyn," Jahir said.

The Naysha nodded. */Frequent guest. She is a good friend. Not all people are comfortable with us, but she has never found me strange./*

Jahir knew about the repulsion some Pelted felt for the Naysha, whose bodies and faces were just a little too human, but not quite enough, particularly when sheathed in the friction-less skin of a shark and elongated to live in fast waters. Theories abounded as to the source of that discomfort, one that was not as frequently shared by the humans who should have found the Naysha's countenances far more disturbing, but there was no agreement. Only that of all the Pelted created on Earth, the Naysha were the least like their brethren, and known to be the Pelted's prime engineer's personal project. That status set them at a remove that their alien appearances could only amplify.

They were, however, elegant, entirely suited to the environment for which they'd been designed. Jahir could only think them beautiful.

/Are you hungry?/ Paga asked.

He assuredly wasn't, but it was the dinner hour and Vasiht'h would have been the first to remind him that his body was working twice as hard as it should on Selnor. Nor did he think his former physical therapist would accept 'no' for an answer, and when he glanced at the Naysha and found the mischief crimping Paga's eyes, he surrendered to the inevitable. "As if you would allow me to short myself."

/Just testing, alet./

Jahir laughed. "Yes. I am certain."

/This way then./ Pausing at the edge of the pool, Paga added, */You do not ask about the water-sharing./*

Thinking of the Naysha's response earlier, Jahir said, "All things in their time, and everything for its reason."

The Naysha laughed with his fingers on the water, tapping. Then, with a snap of his wrist, */Yes. Come./*

The seawater egress brought them onto the beach, where Jahir should have been unsurprised to find vendors catering to both Naysha and any bipeds in their company, and yet . . . he was surprised. Because even anticipating the Alliance's aims and habits, he was not equal to the task of imagining how they would execute them. But they had created a clever artificial tidepool, deep enough for the Naysha to enjoy, with seating built into its sides for visiting Pelted; in places they had dug tables into dry sand and sealed half its seating so that both Naysha and bipeds could eat together, the one floating with elbows propped on the table, the other sitting beneath the water level. It being evening, the beach was lit, not with the multicolored lanterns Jahir had been expecting, but with small pinlights hidden in the throats of night-blooming flowers and amid their leaves. The delicate petals tinted the lights in a variety of striking colors, and the illusion that those blossoms were emitting both light and their perfume charmed him.

At one of those tables, Jahir enjoyed as light a meal as he could contrive with his former physical therapist looking on, which meant grilled fish marinated in citrus and soy sauce, set on a bed of julienned salad greens, radishes, and some exotic vegetable he could not identify but that felt cool and watery on the tongue. He and the Naysha talked of Mercy, their respective works, the neighborhood. They did not, Jahir noted with interest, speak of his partner, though Shellie Aralyn could not help but figure largely in his life and, particularly, his job.

They returned to the apartment after the meal, though Jahir paused for a long moment at the channel leading under the beach to the row of portals. Behind him, the silver light of stars rode the ocean's dimpled waves, and he inhaled deeply of the complex fragrances brought on the wind that blew soft but constant off those waters. When he pushed himself through the portal, he found Paga waiting, head cocked.

/Still love the waters,/ the Naysha signed.

"Always," Jahir said.

The other nodded. */You are ready for the sharing?/* A grin. */Not too full, nor too uncomfortable? Need break for necessities?/*

"I am ready."

/We do this with touch, I assume?/ The Naysha extended a hand, palm up, the webbing loose between his fingers.

"Yes," Jahir said, and took those fingers. He need no longer fall so easily into another's mind, not with the practice he'd had in Vasiht'h's company and with their countless clients. But he chose, this time, and with the touch of those slick fingers with their slight claws on his, he willingly fell forward . . .

. . . and was caught, in a whorl of bubbles that tickled his bare abdomen, and this was . . . the first and the last of the sensory impressions he received, because what he fell into, past, as through the surface of the sea was . . . an embrace, a rightness, a connected-whole-soul-cradled sense more sublime and urgent than poetry poured like song through a joyous heart. Perhaps he was aware of swimming, of water, of being supremely suited to the world around him, of darkness like wavering curtains in oceans deep and shards of sunlight broken on a high and watery ceiling. Or of swaying, enfolded in a patient and endless now, among strands of seaweed tall as the columns of an undersea palace. Or chasing prey and laughter, and catching both.

But none of it overrode that simple and indefinable and imperishable peace. He existed, and existing, was consonant with the world.

Paga drew him out of the communion with commendable gentleness, and still he gasped, breath drawn tight in a chest already constricted by Selnor's weight. The Naysha made as if to set a hand on his breastbone and let it hover there, without touching. When he was certain Jahir had resumed a more normal respiration rate, the Naysha took his hand back so he could sign, */Yes? All back?/*

"Yes," Jahir answered, voice rough and soft.

/All right?/

He managed a laugh. "As much as possible." Wistfully: "Is it always thus for you?"

Paga's mouth pulled into half of a smile, exposing his sharp teeth and evoking visceral memory of eating fresh from the current, blood and flesh. /Not always. But often. When I am away from work, and no longer focusing on quick matters, thinking things. I float, and let it all float from me. That is the blessing of water./

"Yes," Jahir said. "Even I have found it so, and I am not designed for it as you are. And how you are!"

Paga grinned then, cheeks mounding. /Yes. Shandlin great genius. Did good work on my species. Now you sit back in the water, and I will bring you wine./

"I don't . . ."

Paga eyed him over his shoulder, and that expression leveled by someone with eyes the size of Jahir's fists was . . . moving. "Very well," he said meekly.

/You abuse my hospitality otherwise,/ Paga said, signing with his arms lifted as he swam to the counter of his water-accessible kitchen . . . which included, to Jahir's bemusement, a pantry that the Naysha rose to reach with fins balancing his upper body against the ledge. From it he brought down a squat blue bottle, and the liquid poured from it ran clear into two cups. Paga placed these on the ledge beside them. /Here. Try. No fears. It is more refreshment than intoxicant./

The cups were simple clay; the wine, such as it was, so mild it was reminiscent of Nuera's verjuices, and more delicate by far. "What is it?"

/Made from seaweed,/ Paga answered. /Very thin membrane that sits on the surface of the deep ocean water. Not very intoxicating, which is what I prefer. Shellie also likes it. With popcorn./

"Popcorn!"

/I tell her it's ridiculous,/ Paga agreed with a snort, signing between sips. /Not just to eat popcorn with wine this expensive, but also to eat popcorn here. Gets on the water, looks ridiculous, floats everywhere. And the kernels get trapped between her teeth, and she complains./

Jahir chuckled. "We don't always do the most advisable

things, do we."

/No!/

"At least it is a minor vice. . . ."

/You can say. You're not the one changing the filters because they have popcorn stuck in them./

"And have you changed many such filters lately?"

Paga paused, eyes narrowing. In a Naysha, that involved not just the lower eyelids the species shared with the rest of the Pelted, but a nearly transparent layer as well. Jahir watched it glide over the iris by the reflection on its edge, remembered himself and his manners. "If I intrude . . ."

The Naysha huffed and set his cup down. /Therapist./

"It is my work."

That won him a smile, if a touch grimmer than Jahir liked to see. /I worry. She does not shirk, and smiles, and laughs, but it is only on the surface./ He grimaced, looking down, spreading his hands so that the sentences felt alienated from one another, the words pulled apart. /Don't like the thought of burn-out. She is my partner of many years, and my friend./

"And she won't talk to you," Jahir murmured.

/No./

"Was there some difficult case recently?"

The Naysha shook his head. /Nothing I noted. But maybe she had her reasons for finding something distressing, reasons I would not share. Life experiences. The meaning of things changes, based on who you are./

How true that was. Jahir said, "Perhaps you both need a break. When was the last time you had a vacation?"

The Naysha wrinkled his nose, the thick, frictionless skin folding up near the nostrils over the streamlined bridge in a way Jahir found unlikely. /Don't recall. Not a bad idea./ Shaking himself, he sighed. /Nothing to be done today. Let it drift. We will talk of other things. When was the last time you took a vacation?/

Emphasis in sign was amusing, speed and jerky motions. "As a matter of fact, a year ago."

/Oh? This good story?/

Chagrined, Jahir said, "You have no idea."

Later that night, reclining on a bed he found surprisingly comfortable for a mattress made out of gel tucked into a false rock ledge, Jahir thought of Shellie Aralyn, and her partner Paga, and all the work they'd done with him when he'd been failing of his duties at Mercy in a desperate bid to surpass his limits. He had not so done—had in fact discovered that he had limits, and they were insuperable—but the matter had needed external observation before Jahir had been willing to admit to the futility of his quest. How the mind could lie, and cruelly, without friends to check it! And how difficult it was, deciding who to trust, and learning how to receive their advice at one's most vulnerable moments.

Resting his cheek on his folded hands, Jahir frowned, and listened to the water slapping gently at the ledge below his loft.

———∞∞∞———

In the morning, Paga invited Jahir back to the hospital through the commuter tunnel, but he demurred. "I should like to shop in the city proper," he said. "I had so little opportunity to explore Heliocentrus while at Mercy."

Paga eyed him. /Sure of yourself?/

"I am stronger than I was," Jahir said. He smiled. "I swim daily."

The Naysha snorted. /Far be it from me to suggest waters can't heal. You can take the lock to the seaside . . . there are Pads there, somewhere. Follow the signs./

His bag went into a waterproof sheath, which he handed back to the Naysha on the beach. After promising to stop by the hospital before his departure from Selnor for a proper leavetaking, he used the facilities by the water to freshen up and dress, and then took the Pad to Heliocentrus's city center. There, standing beneath an awning out of the way of foot traffic, he looked up into the skyline of the Alliance's winter capital and found it staggering, with its shining buildings throwing bridges and walkways against the blue sky and hanging gardens full of riotous greenery sculpted into terraced plazas on which places of business and housing developments sat in serried ranks overlooking ponds and parks. Jahir had by now seen enough of the Alliance to have a sense for its aesthetic, but Heliocentrus was one of the twin seats of its power, and its beauty was surpassed only by its size and wealth, and not by much. He could not imagine living here amid such bustle, and yet, how livable it was!

He wandered down to the nearest park, at perhaps a slower pace than he would have employed on Veta, but though he was conscious of the gravity pressing on his shoulders it was far less oppressive than it had been on his first visit. He really was stronger, if not, he thought ruefully, so strong as to push himself. He had learned that lesson well. But he could browse the capital's many curio shops hunting for clever presents for his many friends and acquaintances, or his partner's, and stop for a delightful lunch at a café specializing in local fare—quite literally, from a rooftop garden on the building in which it occupied a second floor corner suite. Its balcony was so extensive most of its tables were on it, and Jahir lingered, people-watching, for from that vantage he could see both the people below him on the street and the people above, walking along one of the high tiers of a terrace. Heliocentrus in spring smelled of tropical flowers, and the sea, and was warm enough to suit even him.

As pleasant as his perambulations were, his flight left in the evening and he could not wish to tarry, given his plans. He made one final stop, at the inevitable coffee shop that sold the concoction thrust on him by Paige, and exited with a bag, which went with him to Mercy. There, decorated with a guest pass, he was allowed behind the doors of the acute care ward, and came upon a round-eyed Tam-illee, her data tablet lax in her hand. "Good Iley Everlaughing!" Maya FirstOnSite exclaimed. "I can't believe my eyes!"

He said, "Alet, I find you working the afternoon shift yet. Have you not left that stool since my departure? I beg you to tell me you occasionally go home."

She burst out laughing. "Oh my *goodness*! Thank the god it's been quiet! Come on, let me take you back!"

He had the great pleasure of pressing an urn—a very large one—of hot buttered coffee on Paige Nettlesdown, who accepted it while giggling so hard she kept trying to wipe her eyes on her shoulder. Radimir and Griffin Jiron were still on staff, but the latter had just left; Paige immediately sent for him and he arrived as his former coworkers were slicing into the red velvet cake Jahir had bought from the coffee shop. The Eldritch had had correspondence with all of them, on and off, through the years that separated him from his residency, but those occasional viseos or letters were not the same as being here, smelling the cold, clean halls and the mingled stimulant-and-sugar aromas of the break-room, and seeing them again in this place that had once laid him so low. But he was no longer that unfortunate, and not a single one of them failed to observe it with happiness. It was good to see them, and the acquaintances as well, the on-call healers, even the surgeon Septima, who showed up to squint at him, eat cake, and make gruff noises he knew better than to take seriously.

They came and went, of course, as they were called back to work. He tarried, since he could—he'd set aside several hours for this reunion, knowing the ebb and flow of their duties—and it was during one of those lulls when he was alone in the break-room with his cup of (black) coffee that he was surprised by the visitor he hadn't expected.

"It's all the news," Grace Levine said, with a self-deprecating little smile as she paused by the doorway. "That you came by to visit."

"Doctor," he began, and lapsed when she shook her head.

"Let me," she said. "I just . . ." Halting, and resuming with determination, "Can I show you a picture of my family?"

"Your family?" he repeated, but she was already advancing, bringing her hospital-issued tablet from her coat pocket: a hand-some human man with skin a warm brown, and between them a young boy hugging a plush starship.

"He can't be separated from the thing." Levine sounded irri-tated, but she was smiling at the viseo as she pushed some of her golden hair back behind an ear. "I've had to restuff it twice."

"Did you do it yourself?" he asked, amused.

"Believe it or not." She laughed. "They taught us how to close with catgut thread in this historical surgery elective I took, so I went at it like a head wound in the dark ages."

Charmed, he asked how they'd met (at the hospital; he worked in the billing department), how long they'd been married (almost four years), and whether they were planning any more children (most certainly). He poured her coffee; accepting the offering and the implied welcome, she cut herself a sliver of cake ("not too much though, sugar gives me more headaches post-pregnancy, no idea why"). When the conversation ran down, they both breathed in and addressed one another in unison.

"Doctor—"

"Alet—"

She blushed and said, "I'm so sorry."

Gently, Jahir said, "What for?" When she looked away, her color brightening, he continued, "For sending me away before I broke myself on Mercy's shoals? For your impossible situation, needing to weigh a resident's life against the hospital's patients? For the superlative review you sent home with me, waiving the remainder of my residency?" When she didn't answer, he added, very tender of her feelings, "For the guilt that drove you to confess of yourself to my mentor?"

Her head jerked up.

Jahir said, "You needn't, alet. Grace. It is all forgiven. I beg you will forgive me my lack of courtesy. I didn't even write you a thank-you note for the performance review."

"Oh!" She covered her face with a hand, let it slide down her face. Her eyes were wet. "I've been waiting for years to say I'm sorry."

"And, I hope, to hear as well."

"I'm entirely sure you're being too hard on yourself. A thank-you note!" Her smile was rueful. "Of course you're forgiven, if you believe you need to be. I don't think you do, but I like to think I'm a little better at noticing and responding to people's needs now. You're not the only person who taught me that, but you were certainly the most . . . um . . . dramatic."

He chuckled. "Little about that situation lacked drama."

She sighed. "Yes." She smiled a more natural smile, and it lit her eyes, transformed her. "Thank you."

"You're welcome," he said, and tapped the plate. "You should finish your sliver of cake, and tell me about how the work goes. I have heard all about your family, but nothing of Mercy!"

They talked for some time then, as people came in and out of the room, until she begged off to return to her rounds. That left him with Jiron, who said after a long pause, "You know, if you'd told me ten years ago that she would settle down as much as she has, I wouldn't have believed it. But she's gotten mellow. It's been good for her."

"I hope the drug outbreak did not scar her overmuch."

"Only as much as it did all of us, you included." The human chuckled. "But no, as much as it would have been storybook-appropriate for the wet crisis to turn her around, what she really needed was a sincere and clumsy accountant with a goofy smile and an enormous heart."

"Love does not solve every problem," Jahir said. "But the ones it solves, it often solves completely."

"You would know," Jiron said, grinning. "And that Glaseah of yours with you. He still as fierce as I remember?"

"Just as," Jahir agreed, amused. "And it is obvious to everyone but himself."

"Isn't that the way!"

And it was. Which was on his mind after he'd taken his leave of the denizens of Mercy to trudge back to the pool to tender his farewells to Aralyn and Paga. How essential an external perspective was, given how often the mind convinced itself of its own reliability. And he wondered . . . but of course, he had not been engaged as a therapist, nor been asked for advice, and to proffer it unprompted was inconsiderate—at best!—but . . . a friend might inquire after another friend's state. Could he not?

When he arrived and Aralyn divulged that Paga was with a

client and should be done shortly, he asked if they might wait in her office. The Asanii eyed him with a lifted brow, then led him back to her door, and inside. "So, what's this about, then?"

"I thought I might ask . . ." He hesitated. "Alet, you seem ill at ease. You need not speak of it to me, but perhaps . . . someone else?"

She stopped as if struck, eyes round and shoulders trembling. "If I spoke out of turn . . . !"

The Asanii held up a hand. "How . . . I thought I was . . ." She scowled, ears flattening against her hair. "I was trying to keep it to myself!"

"Forgive me, but is that wise?"

She blinked, then guffawed. "I guess you would ask that, wouldn't you." Folding her arms, she stared down at her toes, tail twitching behind her. Jahir waited patiently, and as he expected, she finally continued. "It's not any one thing. I'm just tired. We help a lot of people, alet. Some recover fully. Others . . . not so much. Some we have to refer to other practitioners, and some don't make any progress at all. I'm grateful for every day we're here, but there are days when it doesn't seem enough."

"And those days lately are more numerous than any other kind," Jahir guessed.

She drew in a shaky breath and frowned. "Did Paga tell you to talk to me?"

"No," Jahir said. "I decided to, because I thought you looked troubled." At the skeptical look she threw him, he tapped the skin alongside his eyes. "Here. There is tension here, and under your eye. And you look away more quickly."

Now she was staring at him. "That's . . . eerie. Or creepy." And then with a laugh, "Though I guess it's no more creepy or eerie than Paga and I knowing what's wrong with someone just by studying the body mechanics they're not aware of, is it. This is your trade."

"Yes."

She pulled the knee-high ball she liked to roll with her foot out from beneath her desk and sat on it. "I don't feel like I have the right to this much angst. We've had hard cases recently, but we always have hard cases, and they weren't any worse than things we've dealt with in the past." She wrinkled her nose. "Actually, some of the ones we've had in the past were *much* worse. So why now, when I have no reason?"

"The years have a weight of their own, alet. A great gash might be more visible, but a thousand small cuts are no less problematic, particularly delivered in the same place. And the heart of you that beats for this work . . . that is a place that can be wounded."

She looked up at him with a sad smile. "So, healer, what's your recommendation?"

"You need a vacation," he said. "And not a short one."

Her ears sagged. "But there's so much to do here."

"Life will never cease for your convenience, or your health," Jahir said. "You must make peace with the fact that you will have to leave your responsibilities in other hands for a time." At her uncertain expression, he said, "It is why we have a community, alet. Do you not trust your peers at Mercy?"

"Of course! But . . ."

"If you do," he said, "then you must trust them with your health as well as that of your patients. And that means allowing them the opportunity to allow *you* the opportunity to heal. Ask them yourself, and see how quickly they acquiesce to the notion. They care about you, Shellie. They already know you need a break."

"It would be nice," she murmured. "To do something different. I just . . . I don't know what."

Jahir said, "Leave the planet, I should think."

"Leave the . . ."

"How do you feel about beaches?" Jahir asked. "Tsera Nova is magnificent."

"Tsera Nova!" she exclaimed, laughing. "How much money do you think I make!"

"How much have you failed to spend while working here?" he asked, guessing, and—

Blushing, Aralyn said, "All right. Point. But . . . Tsera Nova? Didn't they just have some huge disaster?"

"Almost a year ago," Jahir said. "Which makes this the best time to go, does it not? They are very much on their guard against anything occurring again. The memory is fresh."

"Hah. Yes, I can see that." Her eyes were distant. "But . . . Tsera Nova? Seriously? It's so far away."

"Not so much," Jahir said. "Take Paga with you. He can swim with the native cetaceans."

Aralyn bleated a laugh. "Paga! Swimming with Tsera Nova's whales? I'd love to see that!" She shook her head. "I don't know, alet. I think . . . well. You're certainly right about taking a break. Just . . . I don't know when or how."

Gently, he said, "Alet. Don't wait. And don't stay so close that you will be tempted to come back early."

She glanced up at him, ears sagging. And then chuckled a little, reluctant. "You know the healer personality type well, don't you."

"How not," Jahir said with a wry smile. "I am it."

Aralyn's eyes lost their focus abruptly. "Oh, no. You're *right*. And you ran yourself to pieces and you looked *awful*." Slapping her hand to her mouth. "I'm sorry, that was rude. I just . . ."

"Should not allow yourself to reach that point?" he suggested.

"No!" He mmmed and she laughed a little. "I'm sorry. That really was horrible of me." She rose and pressed a hand to her breast. "I promise you, Jahir. I'll take a break. A real one. And I won't delay."

"Then I am content, and I hope it renews you. I expect it will."

Aralyn smiled, a little sadly. "It certainly can't hurt." She stepped out of her office and said, "Ah, he's done. Do you hear that, Paga? Jahir's extracted a promise from me to take a vacation! He wants you to come, too!"

Paga propped his upper torso against the pool's edge and signed above his head, in broad, enthusiastic swoops: /WHEN DO WE LEAVE??/

Aralyn pressed her hand to her brow, laughing. "Great, now

I'll never hear the end of it until we go."

The Naysha glanced at his friend, and while her eyes were covered, signed to Jahir: /*Thank you.*/

Jahir inclined his head, smiling.

Vasiht'h was awaiting him when he disembarked from the shuttle, bouncing on his paws with an eagerness that swept through the mindline like the rush of wind against the face of a rider on a galloping horse. Jahir reached for and clasped the Glaseah's hand, just to enjoy the fullness of the sensation, before letting it drop and falling in alongside his dearest companion.

"You feel happy," Vasiht'h observed. "How was Selnor?"

"I found it very well indeed. It was good to see my former coworkers."

Vasiht'h grinned. "I'm sure they were glad to see you. Did you inflict buttered coffee on Paige this time?"

Jahir laughed through the mindline, keeping his head down as they navigated the bustle of the port. "Perhaps a little."

Spotting the memory of the urn exchanging hands, Vasiht'h barked a laugh. "A little! That's enough for an entire hospital shift!"

"No doubt she found the wherewithal—or the friends—to finish it."

"No doubt." Switching to the intimacy of the mindline, the Glaseah said, /*And the experience with Paga?*/

Jahir thought of the sense of oneness, of perfect harmony with the world around him, and wondered if he would ever experience it again. Probably not in this lifetime, he thought wistfully, but then . . . his lifetime would be long, and who was he to say what experiences God and Lady had planned for him yet? /*Sublime. I am truly glad to have gone. For many reasons.*/

"Good," Vasiht'h said aloud. "Let's go drop off your stuff and get you fed. I love those people but they don't know how much management you need."

"As you say," Jahir said meekly.

Two weeks later, the post brought a rare piece of physical mail, in the form of a viseo postcard. Vasiht'h looked over his arm and said, "Goddess! Are those your physical therapists . . . at *Tsera Nova*??"

On the card, Shellie Aralyn was sitting cross-legged in the surf, shading her eyes and waving as the water rushed past her, foaming on the sand. Beside her, Paga was lying on his back like a beached whale, holding his hands above his head in a sign: "FANTASTIC."

"Oh my Goddess," Vasiht'h said, laughing. "That *is* the two of them. On Tsera Nova! Did you tell them to go??"

"I thought they might enjoy it?"

"Oh my Goddess!" Vasiht'h wiped his eyes. "I can't believe. . . . Oh my . . . I need to bake something . . . with macadamia nuts . . . you sent your physical therapists . . . to Tsera Nova!"

As the Glaseah staggered toward the kitchen, still laughing, Jahir smiled down at the postcard and ran his fingers over it. "Waters," he murmured to them, "heal." And ambled after his friend, to attach the viseo to their refrigerator door and moderate—as much as possible—his Glaseah's caloric enthusiasm.

APPENDICES

PYNADE CANDY

THERE'S NO GETTING AROUND it . . . the recipe for "Family" has to be pynade, because at the time I wrote the story I went hunting specifically for unusual medieval candies for the Eldritch to have preserved in their flight to their new world. Pynade, which is a pine nut brittle, certainly fit the bill. The source for this one is a fifteenth century cookbook, and included chicken originally (!), which supposedly gave the candy some much needed moisture? Needless to say, the Eldritch version does not include chicken. That's a little too odd, even for them . . . !

Having said that, this is also the one recipe in the entire series I haven't made, because I don't make candy often. Fire likes to burn me, and overseeing pots of boiling sugar makes me nervous. I do it once in a while when I need to make marshmallows, but that's stressful enough without boiling anything to the hard crack stage! So I honestly have no idea what these taste like. I present the recipe to you, readers, in the hopes that a braver person than me might take a whack at it! For the rest of us, well . . . here's a piece of medieval history.

Fifteenth-Century Pynade

- 1 cup honey

- ¼ tsp ginger

- ¼ tsp cinnamon

- ¼ tsp pepper

- ¼ tsp clove

- ¼ tsp cardamom

- ½ cup pine nuts

The list of spices on this varies. Grains of paradise and galangal are also sometimes included.

At this point you have a choice, because people seem to take one of two roads: either they put all the ingredients in a pot together and boil them to hard crack stage (300° F on a candy thermometer), or they put the honey in alone, boil that to hard crack, and then stir in the pine nuts and spices. Whichever method you choose, once you oversee your pot of boiling dangerfluid to 300° F, pour it into a pan lined with parchment paper, or separate candy molds, and let it cool. After that, you can pop it out of the molds, or break the pan-sized piece into bite-sized pieces, and consume!

I bet it would be interesting to toast the pine nuts before throwing them in, just to add a little more flavor. Either way, I bet it's delicious. What's not to like about honey, spices, and pine nuts! Give it a try, if you like candy-making, and enjoy!

THE SPECIES OF
THE ALLIANCE

THE ALLIANCE IS MOSTLY composed of the Pelted, a group of races that segregated and colonized worlds based (more or less) on their visual characteristics. Having been engineered from a mélange of uplifted animals, it's not technically correct to refer to any of them as "cats" or "wolves," since any one individual might have as many as six or seven genetic contributors: thus the monikers like "foxine" and "tigraine" rather than "vulpine" or "tiger." However, even the Pelted think of themselves in groupings of general animal characteristics, so for the ease of imagining them, I've separated them that way.

THE PELTED

The Quasi-Felids: The Karaka'An, Asanii, and Harat-Shar comprise the most cat-like of the Pelted, with the Karaka'An being the shortest and digitigrade, the Asanii being taller and plantigrade, and the Harat-Shar including either sort but being based on the great cats rather than the domesticated variants.

The Quasi-Canids: The Seersa, Tam-illee, and Hinichi are the most doggish of the Pelted, with the Seersa being short and digitigrade and foxish, the Tam-illee taller, plantigrade and also foxish, and the Hinichi being wolflike.

Others: Less easily categorized are the Aera, with long, hare-like ears, winged feet and foxish faces, the felid Malarai with their feathered wings, and the Phoenix, tall bipedal avians.

The Centauroids: Of the Pelted, two species are centauroid in configuration, the short Glaseah, furred and with lower bodies like lions but coloration like skunks and leathery wings on their lower backs, and the tall Ciracaana, who have foxish faces but long-legged cat-like bodies.

Aquatics: One Pelted race was engineered for aquatic environments: the Naysha, who look like mermaids would if mermaids had sleek, hairless, slightly rodent-like faces and the lower bodies of dolphins.

Other Species

Humanoids: Humanity fills this niche, along with their estranged cousins, the esper-race Eldritch.

True Aliens: Of the true aliens, six are known: the shapeshifting Chatcaava, whose natural form is draconic (though they are mammals); the gentle heavyworlder Faulfenza, who are furred and generally regarded to be attractive; the Akubi, large dinosaur-like fliers with three sexes; the aquatic Platies, who look like colorful flatworms and can communicate reliably only with the Naysha, and the enigmatic Flitzbe, who are quasi-vegetative and resemble softly furred volleyballs that change color depending on their mood. New to the Alliance (and not pictured in the line-up) is the last race, the "Octopi" of *Either Side of the Strand*.

For a more detailed look into the species of the Alliance, a Peltedverse Guidebook is available through me; you can get it by signing up for my mailing list (from my website), by jumping on my Patreon, or by emailing me directly (haikujaguar at gmail).

THE SPECIES AND RACES OF THE PARADOX PELTED UNIVERSE

PLATIES

NAYSHA

HEIGHT IN FEET

HUMAN
ELDRITCH
CHATCAAVA
AKUBI
PHOENIX
FAULFENZA
CIRACAANA
GLASEAH
MALARAI
HARAT-SHAR
HINICHI
TAM-ILLEE
AERA
KARAKA'A
SEERSA
FLITZBE

Brief Glossary

Alet (ah LEHT): "friend," but formal, as one would address a stranger. Plural is *aletsen*.

Arii (ah REE): "friend," personal. An endearment. Used only for actual friends. Plural is *ariisen*. Additional forms include *ariihir* ("dear brother") and *ariishir* ("dear sister").

Dami (DAH mee): "mom," in Tam-leyan. Often used among other Pelted species.

Fin (FEEN): a unit of Alliance currency. Singular is deprecated *finca,* rarely used.

Hea (HEY ah): abbreviation for Healer-assist.

Kara (kah RAH): "child". Plural is *karasen*.

Tapa (TAH pah): "dad," in Tam-leyan. Often used among other Pelted species.

ELDRITCH
COLOR MODES

MOST PELTEDVERSE READERS will be familiar by now with some of the conventions of the Eldritch language; particularly that of shading words with colors meant to inflect their meanings. In the spoken language, these moods are indicated with single-syllable prefixes; in the written, with colored ink if people want to bother with them. (And as we learn in other books, the color modes are carried into other formats, like music.)

The seven modes come in three pairs, with an added neutral mode, and are as follows:

◈ *Gray* is the normal/neutral mode, and requires no prefix. It has one, though, if one wants to be obvious about one's neutrality.

◈ *Gold* is the best of all worlds, and foil to *Black's* violent, angry, dire, or morose connotations. This pair is the extreme emotional end of the spectrum, good and bad.

◈ *Silver* is the positive, hopeful shading, foil to *Shadow* mode, which gives negative (cynical, sarcastic, ironic, dreadful, foreboding, fearful, etc) connotations to words. If gray is in the middle of the spectrum, black and gold the ends, then shadow and silver are between them and the gray fulcrum.

◆ *White* is the mode for holy things; its foil is *Crimson*, for things of the body. (If you want to be technical, Eldritch illustrations put it on a perpendicular line from Gold/Black, with gray still in the center: white above, crimson below.)

Eldritch is an aggressively agglutinating language: if it can make a word longer by grafting things onto it to add meaning, it will, and if that makes it harder for non-native speakers to pronounce anything without stumbling, so much the better. It's also fond of vowels, and almost inevitably if you see an Eldritch word with more than one adjacent vowel, they're pronounced separately. There are also no "silent" vowels (so Galare is not 'Gah lahr', but 'gah lah reh' or 'gah lah rey' depending on your regional accent). There are some cases where I've misspelled things, or I've continued to write out diphthongs instead of using diacritics, but for the most part if you pronounce every single letter you see in an Eldritch word separately, you'll probably be doing it right.

Like many of the languages of this setting, Eldritch was originally a conlang, created by the people who would become the Eldritch as a way to set themselves apart from the people they fled. It has been several thousand years since then, though, and the language has only become more convoluted since, a reflection of its people's needs.

Author Sketches

It's typical for me to do sketches while writing, a sort of mental doodling as I work out events and character arcs. These sketches are not intended to be the final word on what the characters look like! In fact, I usually have trouble pinning down people's looks. I just keep at it anyway.

Jahir and Vasiht'h are among some of my oldest characters, and the art for "Family" in particular is from a long time ago, since the bones of this story were put down long before any of the rest of the series. (Yes! I wrote the last story first!) Needless to say, there's a lot of art of them that's not up to my current standards—some of the earliest are from the '90s! Nevertheless I have braved the archives, and here are my favorites of those ancient drawings.

1. **Jahir and Vasiht'h on the (First) Couch:** Check out Vasiht'h in his fancy vest-and-blouse with House token! He looks handsome. I actually like this picture, if it wasn't for the fact that Jahir didn't keep a pointed face . . . his character design evolved toward the squarer neckline that gets mentioned here and there throughout the series. I don't know what to tell you about that bizarre chair arm, though.

2. **Fancy Coat:** As you can see, most of my early art of these two involved a lot of very complex clothing. This one is even in my files as 'fancycoat'. You can tell what mattered to me. *grin*

3. **Jahir and Vasiht'h on the (Second) Couch:** This one is even older than the first couch picture. I like it because it's got an honest-to-goodness meander tabard in it, like the one Reese encounters in the Her Instruments series.

4. **Ghost of a Girl:** That's supposed to be Sediryl in the back, there, but like everyone else she evolved a lot. This version of her is too voluptuous (for an Eldritch) and has the wrong hair. Also, Jahir peacebonding a dagger? Or relieving it of its peacebonding? Not sure which. What was I thinking? It was so long ago I couldn't tell you. But it's one of the first pieces of the three of them together.

5. **Sediryl, Angles:** This, though, is the first drawing I did of Sediryl, and it's the one from which all her subsequent character design evolved: sensual, vibrant, assertive. And young.

6. **The Cup:** A rare piece that illustrates a scene that stayed the same through all the drafts of the story, so I couldn't not include it.

7. **Paga and Aralyn:** Finally, a couple of pieces for the short story, Healing Waters . . . here's Paga and Aralyn, and above them, the "seating arrangements" for the tables in the beach.

8. **Paga's Apartment:** Facing outward, the clear hemispherical view.

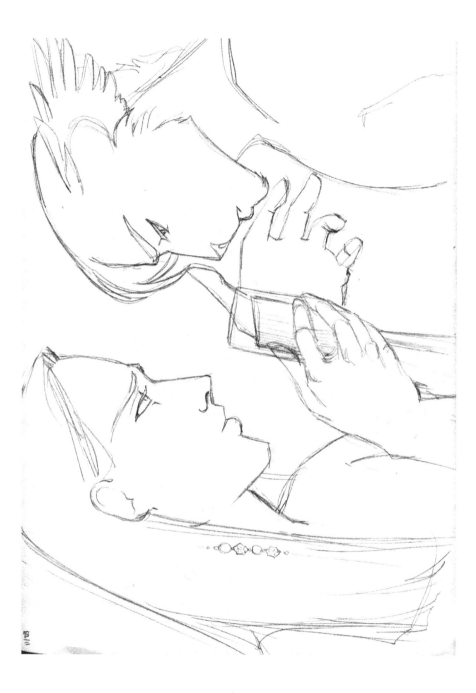

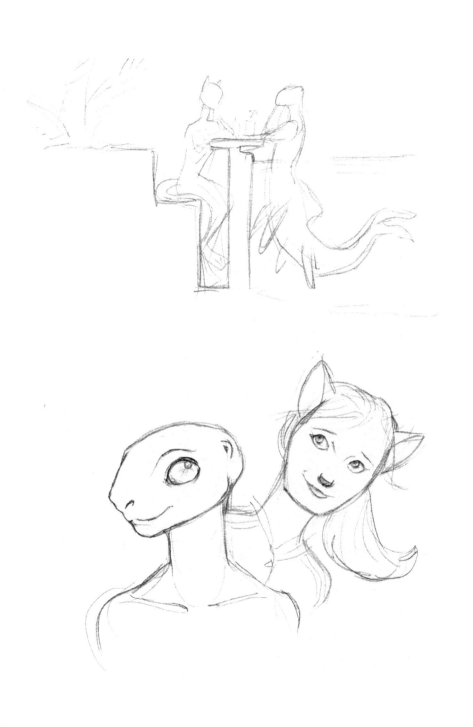

RETURN TO THE ALLIANCE

As with every other book in this series thus far, I end with an invitation to further explore the Peltedverse, and my other series. By now you've had the run-down, so I will simply remind you. For more Eldritch, in an adventure vibe: begin with *Earthrise* (Her Instruments 1). For more Eldritch, in an epic war vibe: go for *Even the Wingless* (Princes' Game 1). For an assortment of shorts, you will want *Claws and Starships;* if you want to wander through the Pelted Fleet, Alysha Forrest is your guide, and you may begin with her dark prequel, *Alysha's Fall,* or the more amiable *Second,* another forever-friendship story.

If you've burned through the Peltedverse, I invite you to check out the rest of my catalog, which you can see in its entirety on my website, at the books page. I have something for everyone, from epic fantasy and military science fiction to lyrical romances. There might even be some business books, kid's fiction, and coloring books too.

More Pelted stories are forthcoming; the best way to keep track of them is to join my newsletter (follow the link from my website, mcahogarth.org). Or you can hop on my Patreon (mcahogarth there as well) for excerpts and sneak peeks, or keep an eye on my twitter (mcahogarth) for announcements.

Thank you for reading!

—M

ACKNOWLEDGMENTS

ONG-TIME FANS WILL RECALL that "Family" was actually the first story ever written about Jahir and Vasiht'h; not only the first, but the story you've just read is actually a second draft of it. The first is nearly unrecognizable in comparison, and I'm glad to report it's lost on some forgotten computer hard drive from an era when floppy disks were still a thing. Rest in peace, early draft. You did your job, but we're glad you're buried too deep to haunt us all.

Back when I wrote "Family," though, I thought of it as the only important story about the dreamhealers, because despite evidence to the contrary I'd accepted the common wisdom that science fiction stories must either be adventures or literary pieces. The rescue of the failing Eldritch world was obviously a story . . . the everyday concerns and struggles of two people figuring out their life, not so much so.

But I was wrong. And I should have known better, because one of my favorite stories is a pastoral, the Anne of Green Gables series, and nothing could have been more delightful to me, as a child and again as an adult (and again and again!) than to read the commonplace adventures of a girl growing into adulthood. When people asked me about Jahir and Vasiht'h, and how they met, and how they went on afterward . . . I knew immediately the model I wanted to follow.

So this final book in the Dreamhealers saga, I have two thank-yous. One belongs to Lucy Maud Montgomery, who taught me how to find the whimsical and the extraordinary in the everyday.

The other, dear readers, I extend to you. For asking for these stories, and then loving them so much. I would never have thought to write them on my own, and I would have been poorer for it.

Here's to many more years of unexpected joys.

ABOUT THE AUTHOR

DAUGHTER OF TWO CUBAN political exiles, M.C.A. Hogarth
was born a foreigner in the American melting pot and has
had a fascination for the gaps in cultures and the bridges that
span them ever since. She has been many things—web data-
base architect, product manager, technical writer and massage
therapist—but is currently a full-time parent, artist, writer and
anthropologist to aliens, both human and otherwise. She is the
author of over fifty titles in the genres of science fiction, fantasy,
humor and romance.

The *Dreamhealers* series is only one of the many stories set
in the Pelted universe; more information is available on the
author's website. You can also sign up for the author's quarterly
newsletter to be notified of new releases.

If you enjoyed this book, please consider leaving a review . . .
or telling a friend! (Or both!)

mcahogarth.org
mcahogarth@patreon
mcahogarth@twitter

Made in United States
North Haven, CT
22 August 2024

56449532R00075